STOLEN CHILDHOODS OF THE PEAK

CATHARINE DOBBS
DOTTIE SINCLAIR

Copyright © 2025 by Catharine Dobbs

All rights reserved.

No part of this book may be reproduced in any form or by any electronic or mechanical means, including information storage and retrieval systems, without written permission from the author, except for the use of brief quotations in a book review.

CHAPTER 1

*1*880

Maisie's good mood lessened when she entered the courtyard of her tenement block. There was a lot of shouting, and it echoed around the enclosed space. The walls seemed to hold in all the goings-on in the houses that connected to the courtyard itself.

It made her and her brother aware that her parents were fighting again. Maisie hated it when they did that.

'Maisie?' Noah stood beside her, tucking his books under his arm. 'We're going to have to go inside.'

'Do we have to?' Maisie asked, looking up at their house, squashed in between two other terraced houses that looked identical. 'It's going to be very noisy.'

'I know, but we must do it. We can't stay outside all day.'

Maisie brightened up. 'But we can, can't we? Mother and Father always want us to play outside.'

'Maybe...'

'Then we can play out here for a while, can't we? You said you would join me and Daisy in playing with our skipping rope, didn't you?'

Noah made a face. 'Did I? I don't recall saying that.'

Maisie pouted. She knew her brother was teasing her. He never broke a promise when he made it, not even when it was something like playing with his little sister and her friend when he would rather do something else. If his friend joined them as well, then it would be even more fun. Nathan was good at making everyone smile.

Maisie enjoyed being around him.

'Please, Noah? Please?' Clasping her books to her chest, Maisie bounced up and down on the soles of her feet. 'You said you would!'

Noah groaned. 'Don't do that, Maisie! You're making me sick.'

'Say you will and I'll stop!'

Noah pushed her shoulder, which made Maisie giggle. Then she squealed as he dropped his books and chased her, trying to tickle her. She was fast, but Noah was faster and could keep up with her easily.

He caught her around the waist and lifted her into the air, spinning her around. Thin and gangly, he was already growing tall, so Maisie's feet were easily off the ground.

'Noah!' Maisie screamed, trying not to drop her books and failing, pages scattering everywhere. 'Put me down! Now I'm going to be sick!'

Laughing, Noah put her back on her feet. He grinned at her, the wind ruffling his thick, dark hair. 'I'll play with you and Daisy. I promise. But you'd better not ask me to do it again.'

Maisie snorted at that. 'You will play with us. You always do.' Then she gasped when she saw her schoolwork skittering away across the slabs. 'My work!'

'Serves you right,' Noah chuckled as she chased the various pages around the courtyard.

'You're the one who made me drop them!'

Still smirking, Noah helped his sister collect everything that threatened to disappear in the wind. Then he stacked the books onto the step outside their front door and took off his jacket, which he lay on the ground under the window.

'Aren't you going to get cold?' Maisie asked, shivering in her own coat. 'It's freezing!'

'It's not as cold as you think.' Noah beckoned her over. 'Come and sit with me.'

'Why? It's wet down there!'

'I've got something for you.' Winking at her, Noah brought out a little white bag. 'Sherbet lemons.'

They were Maisie's favourite sweets. She gasped and hurried over, falling into the coat beside her brother.

'How did you get these?' she whispered. 'Mother says we have got no money.'

'Nathan gave them to us. He said you told him about these and how we liked them.' Noah winked at her. 'You can get pretty much anything out of Nathan if you ask him, Maisie. He likes you.'

'Stop it!' Maisie felt herself blushing. 'He doesn't!'

'He's always wanted a little sister. You don't need to be ashamed of it.' Noah held out the bag. 'Take one.'

Maisie didn't need to be asked twice. She delved her hand into the bag and took one of the sour sweets out, popping it straight into her mouth. Eloise Skinner did not know why her children loved sour treats so much, wondering if there was something wrong with their ability to taste anything. Maisie couldn't explain why, but she loved them.

They both tensed as they heard the window above them go up. A moment later, they heard their mother's voice. 'Maisie! Noah! Where are you?'

'Leave them be,' Maisie heard her father say. 'They've probably gone to play with their friends.'

'I heard them a moment ago. And their books are on the step.'

Maisie and Noah both fell silent, carefully pulling their legs back and huddling against the wall. It was like an unspoken agreement to stay quiet, even when their mother was calling for them. Maisie didn't know why they did it, but Noah always led the way.

He told her when it was safe to show themselves, and if he was keeping quiet while Eloise was directly above their head, then Maisie would not argue with it.

'I'm sure they'll be back soon. They're going to be hungry for their dinner.' Charles Skinner sounded as if he were sneering. 'Although they will not get much to eat, will they? Because we can't afford to feed them properly.'

'And who's fault do you think that is?' Eloise snapped back, her voice fading a little as she ducked back into the house. 'If you didn't do what you're doing with our money, we would have more than enough to live on when we're both working.'

'How I handle my money is none of your business, Eloise.'

'We're married, Charles! Weighing each other's business and our money is for us. For our family!'

'And this is for the family as well!'

Eloise snorted angrily. Maisie had heard her like this before, and it broke her heart. Her mother used to be so happy and kind, but recently she was more stressed. And she couldn't stop arguing with Charles.

Then again, Maisie and Noah knew their father did whatever he could to antagonise her. It was like he wanted to make his wife upset. They had to listen to the two of them fighting all the time, and it made Maisie sad.

She didn't enjoy fighting, and she hated it even more that they did it all the time. Eloise seemed to take things badly and her temper was short lately. With her husband goading her about money, it was no surprise. That was all they talked about.

Maisie wished they would stop.

'It will all be sorted soon,' Charles went on. 'I promise, Ellie. You and I won't have to worry about it for much longer.'

'But...'

'You know I don't break my promises, Ellie. I will have it stopped and dealt with soon. You can trust me.'

Eloise snorted, and Maisie didn't catch what she said. She sat up to crane her head over the top of the sill, but Noah tugged her back down, putting a finger to her lips.

'I won't break this one. I'll look after you and the children, even if it kills me. I won't let them get hurt.'

'And if you're not there to make sure of that?' Eloise asked.

Maisie wondered what she meant by that. It was a strange thing to say. What did she mean?

Before she heard anything further, someone called her name. Looking around, Maisie saw her friend Daisy leave her tenement house three doors down and wave at her with a beaming smile.

Noah groaned. 'So much for staying hidden,' he muttered.

There were footsteps inside the house, and then the door opened. Eloise Skinner stuck her head outside, her fair hair falling out of the chignon she had pinned up earlier in the day. She frowned when she saw her children sitting on the ground under the window.

'What are you two doing there?'

'Well...' Noah began, but Eloise shook her head.

'Just get into the house, you two. I'll have dinner ready soon.'

'But can't we play with Daisy for a bit?' Maisie asked, scrambling to her feet. 'Please, Mother?'

Eloise looked as if she was going to argue, but then she sighed and nodded. 'All right. But not for too long. And stay in the courtyard, please.'

Maisie beamed. 'Thank you!'

Her mother's mouth twitched, and a semblance of who she used to be came out. But then it was gone and Eloise bent down, picking up their books. 'Remember, not for too long. It gets dark out here quickly at this time of year.'

Then she was gone, closing the door behind her.

* * *

Nathan could tell that something was wrong as soon as he met Noah at the river. His friend was sitting on the wall, legs dangling down towards the murky waters below. His head was bowed and shoulders hunched. Even when he was having a bad day, he always lifted his head to grin at Nathan as he joined him.

Something was wrong.

'Noah?' Nathan settled onto the wall beside him. 'What's wrong?'

'What?'

'You're looking sad.'

Noah scoffed at that. 'I'm not sad.'

'I know you are. What's happened?' Nathan nudged his friend's arm. 'You were quiet at school today, and that's not normal. You know it isn't.'

Noah scowled, looking like he wanted to tell him to go away, but he didn't. Instead, his shoulders slumped, and he leaned over, almost tipping towards the water.

'Careful!' Nathan grabbed him before he fell off the wall. 'You know you can't swim.'

'At this point, it might be a good thing.'

Nathan stared at him. 'What? Why would you say something as stupid as that?'

'We're in trouble, Nathan.' Noah sounded mournful. 'Trouble, I don't think we can get out of.'

Nathan had no idea what he was talking about. Normally, he would know what Noah meant. They had a code between them, and it was something they shared between themselves all the time. Ever since they were three years old, the pair were close, often getting mistaken for brothers with their similar dark hair and tall builds.

The only difference between them was Nathan's bright blue

eyes and Noah's dark brown ones, plus Noah had a strawberry-coloured birthmark on his chin that made people stare.

But this time, Nathan didn't know what was going on. However, he could tell that Noah was scared.

'How about you come away from the wall and tell me?' Nathan suggested. 'I don't think talking about it here is a good idea. Especially when I can't swim myself.'

Noah snorted and shook his head. But he got off the wall. They started walking down the path beside the river. It was their favourite place to go, away from everyone else.

Most of the river was by the docks, and there was always a strong smell of fish, but when they moved farther away, farther inland, it was quiet and tranquil. It was where Nathan went to think.

And a place where he and Noah could talk. Mostly about Noah's upbringing.

Noah's parents worked on the docks all the time. It was rare for them to have time off for more than a few hours before they had to go back again. And it was simply for pennies.

Nathan was shocked by how bad it was. His parents worked in low-paying jobs, but they were at least allowed to have some time off. Charles and Eloise Skinner didn't seem to have that at all.

Noah and his sister never begged, but they often ended up having food with him and his family. Nathan's parents could have a little more than Noah's family, but it wasn't much. It was enough for Noah and Maisie to have something, though. They needed it.

'What's going on?' Nathan asked as Noah slouched along beside him, hands shoved in his pockets. 'What's happened?'

'Mother and Father were fighting again,' Noah said morosely.

'They're always fighting, though.'

'About money. And it's bad.'

Nathan frowned. 'How so? Is your father gambling again?'

Noah nodded. 'It sounds like that. He's been doing it more and more, and Mother is getting angrier. I can't believe it's getting to this.' He swallowed hard. 'I'm scared that we're going to have nothing left. We'll get thrown out of our home. I heard Mother say we couldn't pay the rent.'

Nathan stopped and stared. 'It's that bad? You're really struggling?'

'Aren't most of the families around here, though?' Noah muttered. 'We're all trying to earn as much as we can.'

'But you're struggling more than others,' Nathan pointed out. 'And your father gambles a lot, so it's no surprise you're having problems.'

'Mother keeps shouting at him about doing it all the time, but Father won't listen. He says that he's going to get a windfall, that it'll stop eventually, and we won't have to worry about it anymore.'

'And he keeps doing it.'

Noah nodded. Nathan had known about these issues for a while now. He had witnessed Charles Skinner taking money from people Nathan had been told not to associate with. His own father dabbled a bit with the horses and Charles was always there at the track, often arguing with the bookmakers after he lost so much money from bad tips about a potential winner.

Nathan didn't like the idea of gambling. The thought of winning money over something risky might sound tempting, but he knew it would devastate people if it ended up going wrong. Charles had been dealing with it for as long as Nathan had known the family. He thought he was good at winning, but he was terrible.

And he didn't seem to care that it was ruining the family. Especially when he gambled money he didn't have or, more likely, wasn't his.

'I'm scared, Nathan,' Noah said, kicking at the stones on the path. 'I'm scared we're going to end up in the workhouse.'

'That's not going to happen.'

'How do you know? If we can't afford to live and we don't have anywhere to go, we'll end up going to the workhouse. I've heard stories about that place.' Noah shuddered. 'You can't leave there once you go in.'

'I'm sure that's not the case.'

'It's easy for you to say. You're not the one who's facing that reality.'

Nathan held up his hands. 'I will admit, it's unlikely for me, but it can still happen.'

'With the money your father earns in his job?' Noah snorted. 'I doubt it.'

Nathan didn't respond to that. He knew that his father had a good-paying job as a solicitor in a firm. He did well, well enough that his family lived in a nice house, in another neighbourhood that was completely different from the one Noah lived in.

They attended the same school and were close friends, but their lives were very far apart. It made Nathan feel guilty for having more privilege compared to his friend. Noah was a smart lad who could easily go a long way, but his parents would never be able to afford the fees to send him to a school that would be ideal for his sharp mind.

It was the same with Maisie, only eight years old, and she was incredibly bright. She would sit and read a book for hours without moving. Nathan had never seen anything like it. She was also very involved in class. While she didn't answer a question out loud unless called upon by the schoolmistress, she listened avidly.

Nathan had to admire that. Not every little child could pay attention like that.

'You'd be surprised. Anyone's fortune can get worse at the wrong moment.'

Noah grunted. He didn't look convinced. He kicked another stone into the river, the water rippling moments after it plopped in. 'Easy for you to say,' he said with bitterness in his voice. 'You've got money and family and all the opportunities of life that I wish I could have. I don't get the same luxuries.'

Nathan frowned. 'Just because my position is slightly better off than yours doesn't mean we can't come crashing down any less hard.'

'You don't know that.'

'My father has told me that since I was little. He said not to take my position for granted. Anything could change and make it worse.'

Noah didn't look convinced. He simply sent Nathan a withering look and continued walking. Nathan had known Noah long enough that he wasn't offended by whatever his friend said. They could argue and disagree on anything, but they would still be close. He loved Noah like a brother of his own and Maisie like a little sister.

They were in a tough situation, and Nathan wished he could do more. He felt helpless whenever he saw someone in need, especially when it was someone he cared about.

'Why don't you and Maisie come over for dinner after school for the rest of the week?' Nathan suggested.

Noah did a double-take, staring at him as if he had gone mad. 'What? Did you just suggest that we should eat dinner with you?'

'Of course. You're always welcome at our home, no matter what. Mother and Father enjoy having you around, and you know you're guaranteed to have a good meal. Especially with Mrs Harman cooking.' Nathan managed a smile. 'You love her cooking. She's brilliant, isn't she?'

Noah bit his lip, and a blush crept across his cheeks. 'What about Bethany?' he mumbled. 'Does she mind having me around?'

Nathan's smile widened. He was aware of Noah's fancy of his older sister. Bethany was fifteen and tended to have her own circle of friends, but she was friendly enough to Noah and Maisie. His sister preferred to be with other people, though. That didn't stop Noah from staring after her and thinking nobody noticed.

Nathan had noticed. He thought it was rather sweet, even if there was no hope for the two of them. It was going to be gone within a few months; he was sure of it.

'Bethany doesn't mind you being there, don't worry. But she spends a lot of time out of the house...'

'I see.' Noah's shoulders slumped. 'Maybe we shouldn't go to your house as much. I don't want to intrude.'

'Don't be silly.' Nathan put an arm around his friend's shoulders. 'You're always going to be allowed into the house. Mother and Father would want to know you two are safe and well-fed.'

As if on cue, Noah's stomach started growling. He grimaced and put his hand against his belly, looking ashamed. 'I...sorry.'

'What for? That you're hungry?'

'We didn't get much for dinner. Mother tried, but...'

Nathan straightened up. 'Where's Maisie?'

'She's playing with Daisy in the courtyard outside the house. Why?'

'Go and get her. We'll go to my house, and you'll be fed properly.' Nathan looked up at the lowering sun, which was starting to disappear behind the trees. 'And I'll get you back before it gets too late.'

Noah still looked unsure. 'But...your family does so much for me already. Me and Maisie.' He chewed on his bottom lip. 'I don't want us to be a further burden to them. We'll be told to keep away if we...'

'Nonsense! Mother would be delighted to see you. You know how fond she is of you and Maisie.'

'Really?' Noah's expression was more hopeful.

Nathan wished his friend wasn't like this. Noah tried to show that he was strong and brave, that he didn't care about anything. But the reality was he was more vulnerable than imagined. He was always focused on looking after Maisie, to try to shield her from the worst of the troubles at home, and yet it always reached her. It was getting to the point that it couldn't be hidden anymore.

Nathan saw the real Noah Skinner. He feared the world, frightened of what would happen. He showed Nathan what was happening, something not even Maisie witnessed, and the two of them had a strong bond. Nathan wished he could help a little more with every passing moment, but there was only so much he could do, especially when Noah was reluctant to take his help.

He did, on occasion, but not much.

'Go and get Maisie and come on over to mine,' Nathan offered again. 'We'll take good care of you tonight.'

'Mother...'

'Will be relieved that someone is helping her with you. She's got enough problems on her hands, and you know your father won't look after you.'

'Mother's gone to work, anyway. She's had to take another shift at the fish guts place, where she must work at all hours of the day.' Noah made a face. 'God, I hate her working there. She stinks when she comes home.'

'And your father?'

'Probably at the racecourse again. He won't be back until very late into the night, banging around on the stairs in the hopes he doesn't fall on them again.'

Nathan had heard it quite a few times, but he was surprised at how much Noah showed his dislike for his father. He couldn't imagine how that would feel for a parent to know that their child hated them.

'Let's find your sister. Then we'll have dinner, and we can play with my toys. How does that sound?'

Noah gave him a small smile. 'Thank you, Nathan. You're a good friend.'

Nathan didn't know what to say to that.

CHAPTER 2

1881

Maisie couldn't sleep. Not with her parents shouting downstairs. They were screaming at each other to the point Maisie thought she would hear their voices echo in her head for hours afterwards.

Beside her, Noah lay snoring away. That would be the noisiest sound in her ears if there wasn't an argument coming from the kitchen, and her father would tell him to shut up.

It was difficult sleeping in the same bed as her parents, but it was all they could afford.

She would not get any sleep now. Not with the screaming. Maisie thought about going over to Daisy's house and sneaking in, but she lived with her parents and four siblings. There was absolutely no room for her there.

Maybe walking by the river would help her feel sleepy. It was nice at night whenever she went for a walk there. The sound of the water gently flowing and the moon illuminating it with silvery light made Maisie wish she could sleep right by the water all the time.

Her mother often told her that she shouldn't be going out in the middle of the night and wandering around as someone might come along and grab her. There were talks of children being kidnapped and taken away for whatever reasons lately. Maisie had heard about it when she was at school. All the other children talked about it, and she had heard the stories.

It was scary to think about, but Maisie didn't want to lose something that made her feel good. She wanted something for herself, a place to hide whenever she needed to. Now was a good time.

Slipping on her shoes and tugging a jumper on over her nightdress, Maisie tiptoed out of the bedroom and made her way carefully down the stairs. She could still hear her mother and father shouting through the closed door.

'I can't believe you did it again! You promised that you would stop!'

Why did that sound like her father's voice? Then Maisie heard her mother.

'How many times do I have to say it before you listen to me? Are you seriously going to bury your head in the sand like this, Charles? We can't keep going on like this!'

Maisie was confused. What did her father mean by Eloise promising to stop? Stop what? That didn't make sense.

She didn't want to hear any more of it. She was close to tears, and she needed to get out of here before she was found. Maisie didn't want any sympathy from them, not when they were the cause.

Getting out of the house without making another sound, Maisie took that opportunity to run. She charged across the courtyard and into the road, darting through the various alleys between the rows of houses. She didn't stop until she reached the river, slowing before she ended up tipping herself into the water. She couldn't swim, and there was no one around.

There was a log that had been chopped down, lying on its side farther down the riverbank. It was a makeshift seat, and that was where Maisie went.

She sagged onto the log, curling her legs up to hug them against her chest. She stared at the water, silver under the moonlight, as she tried to figure out if she wanted to be angry or cry. Right now, she didn't know if she could do either.

'Maisie?'

Maisie screamed as she jumped, and she fell off the log. Landing in a heap on the ground, she looked up to see Nathan adjust his cap, watching her oddly as he held up his lantern. Her cheeks now burning, Maisie scrambled to her feet.

'Nathan? What are you doing here?'

'I had the second shift at the factory, remember? Noah and I work in the same place.'

That was when Maisie remembered. Only six months before, Noah was told that he had to go and find work. They couldn't afford to eat, and they needed his help. In solidarity, Nathan said he would join him. He didn't need to, but Nathan wasn't going to leave his friend.

It was strange not seeing him at school. Maisie missed him, and her spirits lifted seeing him.

'Are you all right?' Nathan peered at her. 'It's very late for you to be out here. What's wrong?'

'I couldn't sleep.' Maisie wrapped her arms around her waist. 'My parents are fighting again.'

'Is it still bad?'

'Yes. I don't know what they're really fighting about, either. I keep thinking that it's money, but there's something else going on, and I'm not sure what it is.' Maisie blinked hard, realising that she was close to tears. 'I don't know what to do anymore.'

Nathan's expression softened. 'You shouldn't have to do anything, Maisie. You're still a child. You're nine years old. You really shouldn't be thinking about stuff like that.'

'That's easy for you to say. You don't seem to have any troubles at all.'

'Are you sure about that?'

Maisie snorted.

'You don't need to work! You do it for Noah. If you had a choice, you wouldn't have to work at all.' She heard her voice hitch, and she stopped, swallowing hard. 'I'm sorry. That was rude.'

Nathan gave her a gentle smile. He was always so kind to her. It was nice to have a friend like Nathan. Maisie always felt her spirits lift whenever she was around him. Of course, it was Noah who was his friend first, but Nathan looked after her as well.

Whenever Noah went to his friend's house for dinner or to play, he took Maisie with him. Those were good times, and Maisie was always happy. Even Nathan's sister Bethany joined them occasionally, and she was sweet.

Maisie wished she had siblings like that. Noah, of course, was a good older brother, but she wished she had more. Charles and Eloise always said they couldn't afford that many children, but they couldn't even manage to maintain two. Maisie wondered why they had children at all.

'Come on, Maisie,' Nathan said, beckoning her to him. 'I'll walk you home.'

'I don't want to go home.'

'Yes, you do. You shouldn't be out here alone. Especially not with children disappearing all the time.'

Maisie frowned. 'But you're a child, aren't you?' she pointed out. 'You're thirteen. That's still a child.'

The light coming from the lantern showed Nathan's smile as he reached into his pocket and pulled out a knife. The blade glinted in the light. 'I always carry this. I'm not going anywhere without it.'

Maisie stared at the knife. It was bigger than the ones her

mother used to gut the fish in the cannery. 'But isn't that going to make things worse? What if someone uses it on you?'

'They can try, but I'm faster than you think. Don't worry about me.' Nathan put the knife away and adjusted his cap on his head. It was strange seeing him in dirty clothes with dust on them. 'Now, let me walk you home, Maisie. It's best that you do. I would feel guilty walking away if something happened to you. I know Noah would never forgive me.'

Maisie didn't know about that, but she could tell Nathan wasn't going to leave her be. He would stay with her when he should be going home. He was always looking out for her.

Even at the expense of himself.

She managed a tiny smile and nodded. 'All right. But don't take me right to the door. My parents are still awake, and they shouldn't see you.'

'They're not going to be upset with me, are they?'

'They'll be more upset with me. Mother told me not to run off during the night.'

'And she's right. You need to go home. Even if things are tough right now.'

Maisie didn't want that, but she didn't have much of a choice. Nathan wasn't going to leave until she did. And she didn't want him getting into trouble for being concerned for her. Sighing and huddled in her jumper, she walked towards him. 'All right.'

'At least it's the middle of May,' Nathan commented. 'It would be far too cold if it was winter.'

'I've done this in winter as well.'

Nathan sighed. 'Maisie, you really...'

'I know, I shouldn't be out alone. How many times have you said it since finding me?' Maisie glared at him. 'I'm nine years old. I can take care of myself.'

Nathan grunted. 'I don't doubt it. But I don't want to put you in a position to find out.' He jerked his head. 'Come on, let's get moving. Hopefully, they've stopped arguing by the time you get home.'

Maisie doubted that. She was surprised that they were able to talk at all, given the amount of shouting her parents did. She wished she could tell them to stop, but they weren't going to listen to her.

Maybe, just maybe, her father would realise what he was doing and stop. Although Maisie doubted that was going to happen.

They went back to her home in silence, Nathan staying close as they walked. Maisie wanted to talk to him, but she didn't know what to say. She couldn't think properly. It was like there was nothing she could say without sounding like a proper fool. Maisie wished she didn't have bouts of shyness around Nathan.

They finally reached her house, and Maisie could see a candle flickering through the thin curtains. As they stood in the entranceway, Maisie caught sight of the door opening and someone stepping outside.

'Someone's coming out of the house,' she whispered. Now she began to panic. 'I can't let them see me. If they know I've been out…'

'Come with me.' Nathan took her hand and tugged her away. 'We can hide.'

They hurried over to the shadows in the next alleyway. Maisie clung to Nathan's hand, shivering as she watched him glance around the corner.

'Someone's just leaving,' he whispered.

'Is it Father?' Maisie asked.

'No, they're wearing a dress. It looks like your mother is going out.'

'Mother?' Maisie was confused. 'But she's not meant to be working tonight. She said that she had the night off.'

'Maybe she's changed her mind. Especially if she needs space from your father for a while.' Nathan turned to her. 'Now will be a good time to try to get inside. I doubt your father would have noticed you gone, but he won't for much longer.'

Maisie swallowed and nodded. He was right. Charles would notice eventually, although she would have a few minutes of grace if she was lucky. He liked to drink until he fell asleep drunk, but when he was disturbed in the process, he could lash out. Maisie feared him when he was like that.

Not that she would admit that to Nathan right now. It would make her seem weak, and Maisie didn't like to think she was weak.

'Off you go, Maisie,' Nathan urged, pushing her gently into the street. 'Go back to bed and try to sleep. You'll be fine.'

'Are you sure?'

Nathan gave him a gentle smile. 'Of course. I promise.'

Maisie didn't know about that, but she held onto the hope. Mumbling her thanks, she hurried back to the courtyard and towards the house. Bracing herself, she walked right toward her home, let herself in, and closed the door as quietly as she could.

Thankfully, no one was in the hallway, but Maisie could hear voices behind the closed kitchen door. Charles' voice was recognisable, sounding morose. The other…

Was that her mother? But didn't Maisie and Nathan see her leave earlier? What was going on here?

Perhaps they had had a visitor over that Maisie and Noah didn't know about when they went to bed. But if that was the case, why would they be shouting at each other? Eloise and Charles never shouted like that with guests over.

What was going on?

Maisie didn't know what to think. She hurried up the stairs, trying not to make a sound, and into her bedroom. Noah rolled over and looked at her with bleary eyes.

'Where have you been?' he asked sleepily.

'Nowhere,' Maisie said quickly, clambering into the bed.

'You've got a jumper on.' Noah rubbed his eyes and looked at her again. 'You've been outside, haven't you?'

'No.' Maisie drew the blankets up and lay down. 'Go to sleep. They've stopped shouting now.'

Noah was silent. Then he sighed heavily, and the bed creaked as he lay down beside her.

'Suit yourself,' he muttered.

As he fell back to sleep, Maisie lay awake and tried to think about what she had seen. Had her parents had a visitor, and who was it? Why did they not know about it?

And was it something to do with Charles' gambling habit?

* * *

Maisie awoke with a gasp as a scream ran through the house. What had she just heard? It felt like it had come out of her dream.

It hadn't, though. It was coming from the real world.

Beside her, Noah sat up suddenly, tugging the blankets with him.

'What was that?' he asked.

'I...what...?' Maisie tried to form the words, but it made her throat hurt. She swallowed and tried again. 'What time is it?'

'Almost dawn. I can see sunlight breaking through the window.' Noah clambered off the bed. 'Where's Mother and Father? They came to bed last night.'

Maisie started to get out of bed, only to get her foot caught in the blankets and ended up face-first on the floor, catching herself on her elbows. Wincing at the pain, she kicked the offending items away and got to her feet.

She ran out after her brother, colliding with his back when she got to the top of the stairs. He was staring at something on the ground floor. Maisie tried to look around him, but Noah turned and attempted to pull her away.

'No, Maisie!'

'Let me go!'

Maisie elbowed her brother in the face and darted around him as he stumbled. Then she saw the sight on the floor.

Their mother lay in a heap at the bottom of the stairs, her clothing in a tangled mess and her head at a strange angle. Her eyes were open, staring at something on the wall. Her skin was white, making her look like a porcelain doll.

And she wasn't moving.

Charles was kneeling by the body, wailing loudly as he grabbed his head and rocked back and forth. He leaned over and reached for his wife's face, but then his fingers merely brushed against her cheek and didn't go any further before he pulled back. He buried his head in his hands as he sobbed.

'Mother!' Maisie charged down the stairs. 'Mother!'

'Stay where you are, Maisie!' Charles shouted.

But Maisie stepped over her mother's legs, clutching onto the bannister, falling to her knees beside her. Now her mother was staring at her, and the sight in her eyes was terrifying. Maisie didn't need to be told that she was dead.

'Come away, Maisie.' Charles reached for her and got up off the floor, moving her away from Eloise. 'You shouldn't have to see this.'

'But Mother...'

'I know, love. I know.'

Charles put his arms around her and hugged her tightly. It was then that Maisie realised she hadn't had a hug from her father in a long time. She couldn't remember the last time he had done that.

She clutched onto him, squeezing her eyes tight shut and trying to figure out what had just happened. Her mother was dead. Had she just fallen down the stairs? Or had she been there for a while? And why had none of them heard it?

'Noah!' Charles shouted up the stairs. 'Fetch the doctor! Quickly!'

'But can we pay him, Father?' Noah asked.

'Don't argue with me. Just get him. Now!'

Charles' voice sounded shaken as he led Maisie into the front room. He urged her to sit down, sagging onto the cushions beside her.

'I'm so sorry, Maisie,' he whispered, hugging her again and gently rocking her. 'I'm so sorry, but…Mother's gone. She's not coming back.'

'But what happened?' Maisie asked. 'Why…?'

'She…' Charles' voice hitched, and he fell silent for a moment. 'She fell down the stairs. Tripped over her own feet.'

But Maisie shook her head and sat back. 'No, that wouldn't happen. Mother is too sure-footed for that.'

Charles blinked a few times, pinching the bridge of his nose. 'I'm sorry, Maisie, but that's how it is. Even those who can stand without swaying can fall and hurt themselves. Or, in this case…'

'So, she's never coming back?' Maisie croaked.

The look on her father's face was enough for Maisie to burst into tears. She started to wail, allowing Charles to pull her into his arms again.

Her mother was gone. And she was never coming back.

CHAPTER 3

*A*s soon as Nathan heard that Eloise Skinner was dead, he ran straight over to Maisie and Noah's house. He couldn't wait around until he knew what had happened. It was shocking to hear that someone as stable and sure-footed as Eloise Skinner had fallen down the stairs. Nathan didn't think that was even possible.

He had to see his friends. They loved their mother, and they would surely be distraught.

It didn't take long to run to the house, only to get there as the undertaker and his assistants were leaving with the body. Eloise had been put onto a stretcher, a sheet draped over her, and as Nathan watched, she was lifted onto the back of a cart.

There was little care going into it, just efficiency. It made him angry seeing these men treat a dead person like that. Charles stood by the cart, his back to Nathan, with his shoulders hunched. Nathan wondered what his expression was right then. Was he distraught or playing the grieving husband?

Nathan knew he shouldn't think so horribly, but he had seen Charles and Eloise together many times over the years, and it had been tempestuous. If he still loved her despite everything, that would have been surprising.

Then he saw Maisie and Noah's neighbours out on their stoops, watching the scene. Little Daisy was clutching onto her mother's skirts, sucking her thumb with a look of distress on her face. That broke Nathan's heart.

Then he saw Maisie and Noah appear in the doorway. Both looked sullen, their faces blotchy from crying. Nathan wished he knew how to get rid of the pain, but he just felt helpless. He didn't like that sensation.

As Charles spoke to the undertaker, Nathan walked over. 'Mr Skinner?'

Charles barely glanced at him, his expression stony. 'North. What are you doing here?'

'I heard about your Mrs Skinner. I'm sorry about what happened.'

Charles grunted and then turned back to the undertaker.

'But surely, you can let me make a payment a bit later?' he asked, sounding slightly pleading.

'I'm sorry, Mr Skinner, but you need to pay me now; otherwise, your wife will be taken care of by the Poor Union. We don't do a service without being paid.'

Nathan couldn't believe what he was hearing. If Charles didn't pay, she would be sent to a pauper's grave? That was horrible.

'My family will pay,' Nathan said before he realised what was happening.

Two pairs of adult eyes turned to him with quizzical expressions. Charles looked bewildered.

'You…you want…'

'If you're struggling, then my family will pay for what you need. You just need to pay them back later.' Nathan silently hoped that his father would agree to this. 'His name is Eric North, solicitor at North and Parker Solicitors.'

'I see.' The undertaker drew himself up a little. 'So, your family will pay for Mr Skinner, will they?'

'Just go along to his offices later today and he'll see you right.'

Nathan could only hope that his father would agree and pay before asking about it later; he cared about Noah and Maisie like they were his own children. If something happened, he would never forgive himself. His father was strict, but he was soft-hearted when it came to his son's friends.

Charles still stared at him as if he were mad. Nathan tried not to shirk back under his gaze. He only thought he was doing the right thing, after all. Finally, Noah's father sighed and nodded.

'All right,' he croaked. 'Thank you, Nathan. I appreciate it. And I'll pay you back for that.'

'If you go to my father, you can discuss it with him. He can write you up a contract.'

Something flickered across Charles' face, but then he nodded briskly. 'Of course. I'll do that.'

Despite his age, Nathan knew how much Charles Skinner gambled and didn't pay people back. He wanted to be sure that he could be held accountable. His father would certainly do that. He glanced back towards the house, looking for Noah and Maisie. 'Are Noah and Maisie inside?' he asked. 'I want to see how they're holding up.'

'They've gone for a walk,' Charles said gruffly, running his hands through his hair. 'Maisie was crying a lot, and I had to deal with the undertaker, so I asked Noah to take her for a while. I think they went down to the river.'

Nathan barely waited to say his thanks before hurrying away. He started to run as he left the courtyard, reaching the riverside faster than normal. Looking up and down the silent path, he couldn't see either of his friends for a moment. Had they walked a long way, or were they hiding?

Then he saw the upturned log he had found Maisie at not even a week ago. Nathan hurried over and found Noah sitting on the ground with his legs stretched out. Maisie was leaning against him, huddled against his side, and Noah held her. She was sobbing quietly into his chest. Noah looked pale-faced and sullen. He looked up when Nathan came around the log.

'Nate?'

'I heard, and I had to come over as soon as I could.' Nathan crouched beside him.

The two friends embraced, and Nathan heard Noah let out a sob. Then his friend stepped back and wiped at his eyes hard.

'I'm so sorry about your mother, Noah,' Nathan said.

'I…I don't know what happened,' Noah croaked. He sounded like he had cried himself hoarse. 'She…she just…'

'I know. It's all right.' Nathan squeezed Noah's arm,

'Father found her first,' Noah said quietly, his tone sounding like he was in a daze. 'He had been doing the night shift at the factory. When he came back, he found her…at the foot of the…'

'Don't.' Nathan pressed a hand to his shoulder. 'Don't say it if you can't. And Maisie…'

'I saw her.' Maisie lifted her head, her eyes shining and her cheeks wet with her tears. 'I saw her body. I know she's dead.'

Then she started sobbing again, which made Nathan wrap his arms around her. He looked close to tears himself. Nathan's heart ached. He couldn't begin to imagine how they were feeling.

And he didn't know how to help them. That was what scared him the most. He genuinely had no idea what to do.

'I…I don't know what to do,' he admitted.

Noah scoffed. 'You don't know what to do? What about us?'

'Well, normally, I'm the one who takes charge. I know how to help you.' Nathan slumped onto the grass. 'And I don't know how this time.'

Noah scowled at him. 'Can you bring my mother back? Can you bring her back to life?'

Maisie whimpered and started to cry harder. Nathan swallowed the hard lump down in his throat, but it didn't go far. It was not a situation he was comfortable with. He hated hearing Maisie cry.

'Your father is dealing with the undertaker at the house. What's going to happen after that?'

'I don't know,' Noah said gruffly. 'Do we carry on as before? Or do we just…get split up?'

'Do you believe you're going to get split up?'

'If Father carries on spending more money than we can bring in, we're going to end up in the workhouse. I just know it.' Noah shook his head. 'I don't want Maisie to be in there. She's not going to the workhouse or an orphanage. I won't let it happen.'

Nathan didn't respond to that immediately. He didn't think he could say anything after that. That was Noah's biggest fear, to end up in the workhouse or the orphanage. Anything that ruined his sister's future. It was all about Maisie.

Nathan could understand that. Someone needed to look after Maisie.

'Noah! Maisie!'

Noah stiffened at the sound of his father's voice. Nathan saw him tighten his arms around Maisie. He looked around and saw Charles walking along the riverside, looking around to find his children.

Noah shook his head. 'I don't know if I want to see him right now,' he whispered.

'You're going to have to,' Nathan pointed out.

Noah took a deep breath and nodded stiffly. 'All right. Stay with Maisie a moment?'

'Of course.' Nathan beckoned the little girl over. 'Come here, Maisie. Your father's coming.'

Maisie didn't initially move, not until Noah stood up. Then she shuffled over to Nathan and hugged him tightly until he coughed from being squeezed. He watched as Noah dusted himself down and waited for his father to reach them. Charles slowed when he saw them and then cleared his throat before quickening his pace to join his son.

'You and Maisie are going with your Aunt Lily,' he said without preamble.

Noah frowned in surprise. 'What? Why are we going with her?'

Charles dusted himself down. 'With everything going on, I won't be able to look after both you and your sister. So, I want the two of you to go to Buxton with your aunt. She's got the space for the pair of you while we recover from this.'

Nathan didn't like the sound of this at all. He had met Charles' sister Lily a few times, and he had never gotten a good feeling about her. There was something off about her, but he couldn't put his finger on it. Maisie stared at her father in confusion.

'But can't we stay at home?' she asked. 'Why do we have to leave?'

'Because I can't afford the three of us to stay in one place,' her father replied. 'And I don't want to worry about you two in the future. I'll send money for your care…'

Noah snorted rudely at that. 'You've never had any money for us in the first place,' he snapped. 'You prefer to spend it on the horses.'

'He does have to earn to pay back my father,' Nathan pointed out. 'My father will pay for your mother's funeral, and then Mr Skinner will pay him back.'

Charles looked uncomfortable at that, and he shuffled from foot to foot. Noah now stared at his friend.

'Did he actually say that?' he asked. 'Your father said he would help pay for the funeral?'

'Of course he will,' Nathan replied, silently hoping that was the case. Easing Maisie off him, he stood up and faced Charles. 'Has your sister agreed to all of this? Only a short while ago, you were arranging for the undertaker to take your wife away.'

'She has,' Charles said sharply. 'In fact, I discussed it with her before the undertaker joined us.'

'We never heard anything about it,' Noah protested.

'She's currently sorting out the house and getting your belongings prepared.'

Nathan felt as if this was something that had been arranged a while ago. This was going far too fast for it to be something they discussed while Charles was dealing with his wife's death. He suspected that something was going on beforehand.

'I don't want to go,' Maisie declared, jumping to her feet. 'I want to stay here!'

'I'm afraid that's not possible, darling,' Charles replied, a look of pain washing over his face. 'Aunt Lily can provide a home for the two of you, and I'll send money to look after you. It'll be a better life for you.'

'Life?' Noah pounced on this. 'You make it sound like we're not coming back.'

Charles seemed to realise what he had said and hurried on. 'Of course you're coming back. It's only for a few months, that's all. Just until I get things stable again.'

Somehow, Nathan didn't believe him. But this wasn't anything to do with him. He was a friend, a child. He wasn't family. It was none of his business.

Even though he wished he was when he saw the reluctant looks on Noah and Maisie's faces. They really didn't want to go.

And Nathan certainly didn't want them to go, either.'

* * *

MAISIE HATED that they were coming out to the town of Buxton. It felt like they were never coming back. She didn't like Buxton, either. It was a smaller place than Derby, but the journey there wasn't comfortable, not in a rickety cart that felt like it was going to fall apart at any moment. She also didn't like the smells coming from the nearby factories.

At least they would have a beautiful view. The Peak District was a stunning place, and Maisie knew how gorgeous it could be at this time of year. Summer was especially lovely. But Maisie had a feeling that she wasn't going to get time to see it. A sensation in her belly said this wasn't right, that something was about to go wrong.

She had been feeling it ever since her father said they were going to live with Aunt Lily for a while. He promised they would come back, but Maisie didn't believe him. She felt as if he was sending them away for good.

Did he not care about them enough? Did he even love them? Or was money more important?

Maisie didn't think she would get any answers out of it.

She held onto Noah's hand the entire way to their aunt's house, Aunt Lily sitting across from them as the cart bounced them around. She kept giving them disapproving looks, but she didn't talk to them, practically sticking up her nose and looking away whenever Maisie glanced over at her.

Maisie had never liked Aunt Lily. There was something about her that made her uneasy. Aunt Lily was strict and narrow-minded. She took everything in her life seriously, and she wasn't very good at giving leeway to people.

Maisie was surprised that her father had even talked his sister into taking his children away. From what she knew, Aunt Lily hated children.

Her mere presence was intimidating. Aunt Lily was unusually tall for a woman, close to six feet in height, and she was also broad-shouldered with a plain-looking face with greying hair tied up into a fierce-looking bun under her hat. She looked like the severe headmistress Maisie had known at her school. But the headmistress had a slight twinkle in her eye on occasion, whereas

Aunt Lily was simply just hard all over. Maisie didn't think she had seen the woman crack a smile at anyone.

How she and her father were close, she had no idea. But Maisie didn't wonder too much about her father. Playing and having fun were more important to her.

She wondered if they would be able to do that in Buxton or if Aunt Lily had something planned for them. She wasn't the fun-loving type, that much was certain. Maisie wouldn't mind too much if she got to go outside and play, explore the countryside. Noah would appreciate it as well.

It was late afternoon, and the sun was beginning to drift towards the horizon by the time they reached the nice-looking and rather large cottage on the outskirts of Buxton. Maisie had never been here before, and she marvelled at how nice it was. Aunt Lily had said that they grew their own vegetables and had a large garden. She hadn't lied about that.

Did she have her own servants? She was in a better financial position than her brother, after all. She had a husband who had a job in finance and did very well for himself. It would make sense if she had servants.

The cart pulled up outside the gate, and Aunt Lily alighted first. 'Come along, you two,' she said briskly. 'Into the house. Bring your bags.'

Noah glanced at Maisie and squeezed her hand. Then he jumped down and grabbed their bags before helping Maisie down. 'It'll be fine, Maisie,' he said quietly, squeezing her hand. 'It's not going to be that bad.'

Maisie didn't quite believe that. But she trusted her brother. He would look after her.

They headed up the path and into the house. The inside was quite spacious, the hallway bigger than the sitting room in her house in Derby. Maisie couldn't help but stare at the surrounding sight.

This was their home? And they were living in a tiny house? How was this fair?

'They're here, are they?'

Maisie looked around and saw a tall, lean man with a trim black moustache and black hair slicked back on his head step out of a room to their right. He was dressed immaculately, looking like someone who could walk into a room and gain attention just with his presence. There was also something about him that made the hairs on the back of Maisie's neck tickle.

He looked them up and down, making Maisie feel uneasy.

'They're here,' Aunt Lily said briskly, beckoning a slightly built young woman who was coming down the stairs to join them. 'Take their bags to their room, Charlotte. And then get them put to work. Dinner is going to be late if we don't hurry.'

'Put to work?' Noah asked. 'What do you mean by that?'

Aunt Lily snorted and sneered at him. 'Did you think you were going to live here and be raised by us? Not likely, Noah.'

'What? But Father…'

'It doesn't matter what your father said to you, young man,' Aunt Lily's husband cut him off. 'You are here to work. Nothing more. After all, you have a debt to pay off.'

Maisie wondered what they were talking about. She was confused. Debt? What debt were they talking about?

Noah looked equally bewildered. 'I don't understand. We're children. What debt would we have to pay off?'

'It's like your Uncle Thomas said, Noah,' Aunt Lily replied with a smirk. 'You're paying off your father's debt. He owes us a lot of money, and the only way we're going to get that back is for the two of you to work for us.'

Maisie's heart sank. She had thought this didn't feel right, and she was correct about that. She felt sad at that. Noah looked outraged.

'So, we got sold like slaves?' he demanded. 'We're going to be worked to pay off what Father owes you?'

'Pretty much.'

'How much did Father borrow from you?'

'That's not for you to know, Noah,' Uncle Thomas said sharply. 'Just know that you're going to have to work. And you're wasting time talking about it when you should be getting on with your chores.'

'But we just got here,' Maisie protested. 'I'm hungry.'

'And you'll get your bread and drippings later,' Aunt Lily snapped. 'Stop whining and follow Charlotte to your room. You haven't got time to be complaining about this. If you want someone to blame for your situation, blame your father. Not us.'

Maisie tried to argue, but Noah clasped her hand. That was his sign to say nothing more. Maisie didn't like it, but she followed his lead.

Because she did not know what was going to happen now. She was scared.

And the only thing stopping her from completely panicking was her brother.

CHAPTER 4

1887

Maisie's hands hurt. She did not know how long she had been sitting outside tending to the garden, but it was long enough that the sun was bearing down on the back of her neck, making it feel like it was burning. Her fingers were sore from holding onto the trowel and fork, and her mouth was dry. She had a headache after being forced to stay out here for the morning.

Lily and Thomas didn't have a gardener. They had let him go shortly after Maisie and Noah came to live with them. Whenever they wanted something taxing to be done, they got either their niece or nephew to sort it out. Even with their lack of experience, in the middle of winter, they were sent outside.

Maisie had asked why they were being told to do it when they could get someone who was more suited to the job, but she had simply been smacked in response and told not to question her orders.

Maisie vowed to never have a garden of her own once she was old enough to have her own home. And even if she had a garden, she would make sure that she could pay for a gardener.

She never wanted to do anything except sit in it once she was able.

Her head was making her lightheaded. Maisie couldn't remember the last time she had a drink. She had simply been told to go outside and get the weeds out of the vegetable garden, almost thrown out while she was sorting out the clothes for the household. Aunt Lily didn't seem to care what she was doing, if Maisie did what she was told.

It made her want to scream. How could her aunt think it was all right to treat her so badly? Maisie hadn't wanted to become her servant, and yet that was how things had turned out. She and Noah were treated even worse than the household staff. Maisie was surprised that they were not completely broken even after all this time. It was terrifying they thought they could treat them so badly, all because of their father's debt.

Now that Noah was nineteen, though, he wasn't abused as much. He had grown rapidly in recent years and filled out to the point he looked like he was a boxer. Uncle Thomas had tried to punish him when he first started growing, and Noah had pushed him away and threatened to beat him if he did that again.

Their uncle had been so scared that they did nothing physically to Noah again. They still mistreated him and forced him to do tasks that made Noah reluctant to do anything.

With Maisie, it was something else. Maisie wanted to scream. She had done nothing to deserve any of that. Why did they think treating her badly was going to get them anything? Maisie wished she could fight back, but she wasn't as strong as her brother.

Her head was spinning, and Maisie lay on the dirty path, staring up at the clear blue sky and trying to not close her eyes. It was hard to stay focused with her stomach churning and the urge to shut her eyes and let the dizziness take over.

'Maisie!'

Someone leaned over her, and Maisie felt hands on her face,

warm and gentle. They stroked her cheeks and put their hand on her head. The person above her muttered something under their breath, and then Maisie felt herself being lifted off the ground.

She was vaguely aware of being carried away before the dizziness clung to her and tugged her into the blackness enveloping her.

When she came to, she was leaning against a tree, the bark digging in her back, and something cold and wet dabbing at her face. Maisie blinked hard. The figure crouched beside her sharpened into focus, and she realised it was Noah. Her brother looked worried as he wiped the cloth over her face.

'You scared me there,' he said, his voice shaken. 'I thought the worst when I saw you like that.'

'I…what happened?'

'You passed out. You've been working out here all evening without anything to protect you and nothing to drink. I couldn't believe it when I heard it from the cook.' Noah pressed something into Maisie's hands. 'Drink whatever you can. Get it down you.'

It was a water flask. Maisie had seen it hung up on the back of the door in the kitchen, something the cook's husband used when he went out into the forest to shoot animals for their food. It was not meant to be touched. The fact Noah had done that was a shock, especially when they knew there would be a punishment.

But from the look on his face, Noah didn't care about that.

Maisie unscrewed the top and drank. The water was chilly and inviting as it slid down her throat. After a few gulps, she felt better. She lowered the flask, but Noah urged her to keep drinking. The flask was almost empty before he allowed her to stop.

'Please don't scare me like that again, Maisie,' he said gruffly.

'I didn't intend to do that,' Maisie protested weakly. 'I didn't realise I was going to be forced outside.'

Noah's jaw tightened.

'You were unwell a few days ago. You weren't supposed to be outside and weeding the vegetable patch. Aunt Lily knows that was something you shouldn't be doing.'

'Someone had to do it,' Maisie croaked.

Noah snorted.

'I overheard her talking to Doctor Maine after he checked on you last week. He said that you were supposed to take it easy and stay out of the sun. That you've been overworked and you're unable to recover because you're constantly working instead of resting. By his words, you should still be resting now, but they're not allowing it to happen.'

Maisie hadn't heard about any of this. She had been told that the doctor thought she was lying about being ill and she had to get back to work. She had been kept away from Noah all day, so people must have suspected the brother and sister pair would talk and find the inconsistencies.

Everyone in the household was just horrible. Even though they did nothing to warrant the disgusting abuse, Maisie and Noah were treated badly. All because they feared Aunt Lily and Uncle Thomas. They were the reason for it, and Maisie knew it.

But to think they were scared that much of someone that they would abuse children. Maisie felt sick knowing she was related to someone like Aunt Lily.

That woman was just a monster. Maisie couldn't believe they were still here. Why hadn't their father come to get them? They had been with their aunt for six years, so they must have worked off the debt by now. How was it possible they were still here?

'I wish Aunt Lily would just leave me alone,' she said, taking another gulp of refreshing water. She still had a headache, but she felt a little better. 'I don't understand her hatred towards me. She's never been like this before.'

'I don't understand it, either, if I'm honest.' Noah scowled. 'We're meant to be family, and she behaves like this? Father must know what she was up to.'

'Has he replied to your letters?'

'No, he hasn't. I can't get a reply from him on anything.'

Maisie frowned. 'Do you think Aunt Lily or Uncle Thomas are intercepting your letters, and he doesn't know about this?' she asked.

'You think they're not allowing us to contact him?'

'There's that possibility. I wouldn't be surprised if they were doing that.'

Noah didn't look happy with that. 'Neither would I. They don't want either of us to contact Father and tell him what's going on, I'm sure. But Father must wonder what's going on. He should come up to visit us.'

'Maybe they're writing back and saying we're busy and unable to respond. That we're doing fine, and he doesn't need to worry about anything.'

'As if Father is going to believe that.'

'He's not that bright, Noah. We both know that by now. I think he would believe anything his sister told him.'

Maisie felt bad about saying that about her father, but she had concluded that he had no backbone. He was easily led and did whatever he was told. Aunt Lily could tell him anything and he would believe it. It was a situation Maisie could believe.

The fact he hadn't come to see them in six years was telling. Both she and Noah had written to him, wanting him to come and get them, that they didn't want to be there any longer. Maisie had certainly detailed the abuse she had been given. But if their letters were being intercepted...

He wouldn't even know the truth.

Maisie's eyes stung, and she rubbed at them. She would not cry.

'Oh, Maisie.' Noah moved to sit beside her and put his arms around her, hugging her tightly. 'I'm sorry.'

'Why are you sorry?'

'Because I can't protect you. I haven't been able to do that since we got here.'

'It's not your fault.' Maisie looked up at him. 'It's never going to be your fault. The ones who are to blame are Aunt Lily and Uncle Thomas. They put us in this position.'

'If it was just me, I'd run away from it all and never come back. I don't care what jobs I get because they can't be any worse than what we've dealt with over the years. But because you're here as well, it's not that easy.' Noah's arms tightened to the point Maisie couldn't breathe. 'I would never leave you behind.'

'Noah…' Maisie croaked.

'Oh. Sorry.' He loosened his hold, kissing her head. 'I wouldn't walk away from you, little sister. That's the only reason I haven't left yet. I don't care about the debt; I want to focus on looking after you. Something our father can't even do.'

Maisie couldn't help but smile at that. Noah had been protective of her since they were little, and he always looked out for her. Whenever things got tough with their household, the person Maisie went to was Noah. She knew she could trust him with anything. It made her feel better. Noah would never let her down.

'Why don't we run, then?' she asked.

'What?'

'I'm fifteen, Noah. I'm old enough. We can run away and do whatever we want.'

Noah tilted his head to one side, slowly releasing her. 'Do you think we'd be able to do it?'

'Why not?'

'If it was just me, I could focus on me, but if you came along, I'd be worried about your safety.'

Maisie pulled away and faced her brother with a hard stare. 'You make it sound like I can't take care of myself,' she said sharply. 'I can handle things better than you can, and both of us know it.'

Noah chuckled and scratched the back of his neck. 'You do have a point. So, does that mean you want to leave with me and go somewhere else?'

'Absolutely.' Maisie didn't even need to think about it. She had been adamant about this choice should it come up. 'I don't want to stay here a second longer, especially now it's getting worse. Aunt Lily is becoming more and more cruel to me, and I can't take it anymore. We must have paid the debt off by now. So, we should be allowed to leave.'

'They're not going to allow us to leave,' Nathan pointed out. 'They're going to make sure we stay for good. I think they've gotten used to abusing us, and the rest of the household prefers it as it's not on them. That's why they don't stand up for us.'

Maisie had figured that out ages ago. She was furious that they were on their own. In her eyes, the remaining servants were just as complicit as their aunt and uncle. She wasn't going to stand for it any longer.

She was aware of eyes on them and looked around. Her gaze landed on Charlotte, Aunt Lily's maid, who was standing on the path staring at them. Maisie stiffened. This was not good. Charlotte would tell her mistress absolutely anything regarding her niece and nephew, and she seemed to take pleasure in getting them into trouble. If she had overheard any of their conversation…

Then Charlotte turned and walked away quickly. Noah tensed when he heard the footsteps.

'Who was that?'

'Charlotte.' Maisie groaned and thumped her fist against the tree trunk against her hip. 'This is not good at all. If she heard us…'

'It doesn't matter if she heard us. We're still going to leave. We just have to be sneakier about it.'

Maisie understood that, but she was now worried it was going to be easier said than done.

***

'You're wanted in the master's study,' Charlotte said as Maisie and Noah entered the house through the side door. It was like she had been standing there waiting for them.

'What about?' Noah asked.

Charlotte gave him a haughty look and turned away.

'It's nothing to do with me. He just said you are to go into him as soon as you're back in the house. You shouldn't be talking back and asking questions.'

Then she walked off before Noah could respond, her skirts swishing. Maisie was sure her hair, which was pinned up severely on her head, bounced with her steps. The thought made her want to giggle, but she stopped herself.

Noah sighed. 'I suppose we're going to have to deal with all of this, then.'

'What are we going to say?' Maisie asked. She was worried now. 'Uncle Thomas isn't exactly the easiest person to reason with. He's worse than Aunt Lily.'

Noah squeezed her hand. 'It'll be fine. Don't panic about anything. We'll get through this.'

'Don't panic? Really?'

Noah grunted, leading his sister to their uncle's study, the room where he spent most of his days. Maisie was surprised anyone knew what Uncle Thomas looked like, given he was in the study when he was home or in a neighbouring town or city dealing with business. She had asked what business it was before, but she had been told that it had nothing to do with her and she needed to shut up.

It was annoying that they still treated her like someone who didn't matter to the family. Maisie wondered what life would have been like if they had stayed with Charles. Would they have ended up in the workhouse? He couldn't stop gambling his money away, so it would have been likely.

After years of being with her relatives, the workhouse was feeling more and more preferable. At least they would know what was coming instead of being thrown into the unknown almost immediately.

Maisie's heart thudded in her chest as she walked to the study and squeezed Noah's hand as he knocked.

'Come in.'

Noah glanced at Maisie and gave her a nod. He was doing his best not to be scared, but it was clear he was nervous. Maisie wanted to assure her brother that they were going to be all right.

However, both knew that wasn't going to be the case. It was bad if they were summoned to their uncle's study.

Entering the room, Noah shut the door, and they moved to stand in front of the desk. Uncle Thomas was sitting behind it, head bent as he wrote with an expensive-looking pen that scratched across the paper. He didn't look up as they approached him, and silence hung in the air.

Maisie stared straight ahead, concentrating on her breathing to soothe herself. This was a tactic he had done many times over the years: Uncle Thomas would carry on with what he was doing until he was sure that those before him were squirming and on edge. He had done it several times with Maisie and Noah over the years.

But they had developed a tolerance for it. Both could stand there staring into the distance as they waited for him. They didn't squirm any longer, and Uncle Thomas seemed to realise that. He would take longer with whatever he was doing, all to make them uncomfortable. By now, it had become a battle of nerves.

And Maisie felt some satisfaction that they always won. Uncle Thomas gave in first every time. It would make her giggle if the situation wasn't so serious.

Finally, he put down his pen and looked up, his eyes narrowing at the pair as they stared straight ahead.

'I've heard some disturbing news about you two from Charlotte.' He didn't hesitate in using the maid's name. 'You two are planning on running away?'

'That is nobody's business but our own,' Noah said stiffly. He didn't blink and continued to stare at the window behind the desk.

'You realise you haven't paid back the debt yet, don't you? You can't leave until you have.'

'We've been working here for six years, Uncle Thomas. I think it's safe to say you would have been paid back everything Father borrowed from you; even if it was a penny a day, you would still have got back a hefty amount.'

Uncle Thomas snorted. 'You don't know how big the debt is, do you?'

'Only because you never tell us anything.'

'All you need to know is you're paying it off for him, and you haven't completed your task. You'd know if you had because we would have thrown you out by now.'

Maisie stiffened and glanced at Noah, but he didn't react. He was better at doing the stoic stance than she was.

'But it's been six years!' she protested. 'Surely, we have managed to pay some of it back, especially when you're paying us barely anything.'

Uncle Thomas gave her a disapproving frown. 'You be quiet, Maisie.'

'I'm meant to be quiet, but Noah isn't? You're exploiting me as well!'

'And I'll discuss this with your brother, man to man.'

Maisie could feel the anger building. That was another thing he did that she hated. He treated her like she was less than nothing and only conferred with Noah. Her brother knew this, too, but there wasn't much he could do about it, either.

'Given that I'm the one who's now getting most of the abuse due to the fact Noah can physically fight back, I think I have a right to protest the treatment.' Maisie stepped forward, only to have Noah tug her back. 'When Father sent us to you, I'm sure he didn't expect his children to be treated so badly.'

'Your father knew exactly what he was getting himself into when he sent you two here,' Uncle Thomas said icily. 'He will not be on your side. In fact, he'll be begging you to fall in line and finish helping him pay off his debt.'

'You mean the debt he should pay off himself?' Maisie shot back. 'He's too cowardly to give up gambling, so he makes his children do it! It's been six years now! We're done!'

Uncle Thomas regarded her with a bitter expression. Maisie felt a shiver down her spine, but she did her best to ignore it. This was something she would not give into. Uncle Thomas could intimidate her as much as he wanted, but Maisie wouldn't allow it.

'Given the situation and the fact you two are becoming more and more defiant as you get older, I think we're going to have to change things around a little.' Uncle Thomas nodded at Noah. 'You're going to work in the quarry. Starting tomorrow.'

Maisie gasped. Noah looked outraged.

'What? You're going to send me to your quarry?'

'That means you're going to move into the rooms meant for the quarry workers. That way, you won't be at your sister's beck and call when she's meant to be carrying out her chores.' Something flickered on Uncle Thomas' face. Was he trying not to smirk? 'You're more than old enough to work there, and you'll be set to work blasting the stone. Meanwhile, Maisie is going to be permanently put to work in the kitchen gardens. Nobody else is going to look after it, not even the gardeners. It's all especially for her.'

Maisie's heart said. Her uncle knew she didn't care to work in the garden. This was his way of exploiting what she hated.

'That's not fair!' she cried. 'You're going to make me work out there?'

'All weathers, all day. Doesn't matter if it's too hot or you're freezing to death. She'll be looking after the gardens and making sure the vegetables grown are picked at the right time and brought into the kitchen. She'll also be going to market to help sell the vegetables and bring the money back to us.'

Maisie couldn't believe this was happening. She hated going to the market. She had done it a few times before, and having so many people coming up to her demanding something while she haggled with them had been overwhelming. Then someone had stolen from their stall, and Maisie had been beaten for it, even though it wasn't her fault. Aunt Lily had said she was pathetic and useless.

She didn't want to do that. It had been too much for her, and Maisie vowed never to do that again. Her uncle and aunt knew that after she protested, so now they were using it to punish her.

'That's not fair!' she shouted.

Uncle Thomas scowled. 'You will not shout in here, Maisie,' he snapped. 'You either talk reasonably or not at all.'

'You know I'm not good at something like that,' Maisie continued, ignoring his warning. 'I hate having to deal with so many people who think they can take advantage because I'm a girl and a child. Are you looking to lose money for taking things to market? Because you will if I do that again.'

Uncle Thomas' eyes narrowed. 'You will not be going on your own. I will be there, or your aunt. We'll make sure you do as you're told.'

'No!'

'You don't have a choice. Besides, this is better than the alternative. We could split you up completely and put you on opposite ends of the country. You'd never see each other again.'

Maisie felt very cold at that.

Noah growled. 'You wouldn't dare split us up,' he said in a low voice.

'Oh, but I will. I intend to do it if you carry on like this.' Uncle Thomas said back, lacing his fingers over his stomach. 'If you don't want to go with the alternative, I suggest you shut up and do as you're told. Because any further infractions, you'll be down in Cornwall working the mines there while Maisie will be sent to the Outer Hebrides in Scotland. I'm sure we'll be able to find her something that will ensure she never comes back to England.'

Maisie wanted to scream. She wanted to throw something, anything, preferably at her uncle. He was threatening her with that? They were already in a dire situation, so why would he force them into that?

'Do you understand?' Uncle Thomas said, his tone dangerous. 'You see where you both stand in this situation?'

'We understand,' Noah replied gruffly.

Maisie didn't say anything. She couldn't without saying something that would ruin their current situation. She simply glared at her uncle, who either didn't notice or didn't care.

Then he sat forward and picked up his pen again. 'Now, get out. Both of you need to get yourself prepared for your jobs. And consider yourselves lucky.'

As she left the room, Maisie felt anything but lucky.

CHAPTER 5

Maisie waited until she was sure everyone was asleep before slipping out of bed. The night was warm, and she heard an owl hooting somewhere in the trees outside her open window. Sweat trickling down her back.

But she still felt cold. She had been trying to get warm all day, and it was becoming cumbersome. Maisie couldn't stop thinking about her uncle's threat to separate them if they continued with their behaviour. He knew they didn't want to be separated, and she was aware he would follow through on his promise to take Noah away.

She couldn't let that happen. She had lost her mother and, her father. She couldn't bear to lose Noah as well. He was her only genuine family now. Aunt Lily was meant to be blood, but the way she behaved said she didn't care about that at all.

They had to do something. But what? Maisie did not know what to do.

She did her best to avoid the floorboards she knew that creaked as she tiptoed down the hallway. Noah slept in a room with two other male servants at the far end, supposedly so they could keep an eye on him. But they were very heavy sleepers, and

Noah had developed the knack of leaving the room without waking either of them. They could claim Noah slept all night because they were too ashamed to admit they had fallen asleep watching him.

Maisie had the same thing but with Charlotte. The older woman was very smug about watching over Maisie, but she was even worse. The woman snored, which made it practically impossible to sleep most nights.

It also helped when she needed to sneak out to meet her brother.

The door to Noah's bedroom opened as Maisie approached it, and she stopped to fight back a gasp as a dark figure slipped out. It took her a moment to realise it was her brother. He put a finger to his lips to indicate she needed to be quiet, and then he pointed to the door that led down the stairs the servants used all the time. It went to the kitchen and right out into the garden.

Maisie followed Noah down the stairs and into the garden. Feeling the cool grass beneath her bare toes was a soothing sensation. Maisie liked the feeling, and she dug her toes into it with a sigh.

'How are you feeling?' Noah asked, keeping his voice low. 'How are you holding up?'

'I'm feeling angry, upset, distraught…' Maisie sighed, and her mood dissipated even more. 'I can't believe he thought to separate us like that.'

'Well, he wouldn't be able to do that. He won't get that far.' Noah sounded adamant about that. 'It's not happening.'

Maisie nodded.

'I agree. But how are we going to change that? They're aware of us planning to run away now, so we're going to be watched even more. They will not let us sit down and have a moment without wondering what we're doing.'

'And they'll make sure we don't interact again. I'm being moved over to the quarry tomorrow morning.'

Maisie felt the tears building. She wanted to cry, but she stopped herself. She couldn't do that. It would just make noise, and that was the last thing they wanted right now. If anyone caught them, they wouldn't be able to see each other again.

'I want to go home,' she whispered, wrapping her arms around her middle and pacing around the lawn. 'I can't stay here any longer. It was bad enough when we were being treated less than people, but forcing us into doing work that will probably kill us...'

Noah raised an eyebrow. 'I know I'm going to be handling dynamite, but how is working in the kitchen garden dangerous?'

'You saw what happened to me today! Do you think I'll be able to cope if they make me do that all day? And, knowing my luck with gardening, I'll end up bringing up something that was supposed to remain in place. Then I'll get beaten for it.' Maisie flinched as she remembered the last time. 'I won't be able to take it if this continues.'

Noah didn't say anything, and Maisie turned to see his face. He looked like he was close to tears as well. Seeing her older brother close to crumbling made Maisie wish she knew what they could do.

'How are we going to get out of this?' she asked. 'How can we leave when you'll be at the quarry, and I'll be here? They'll intercept our letters, I'm sure of it.'

'We'll figure it out. We always do. But we can plan tonight.'

'Plan? How?'

Noah took a deep breath and let it out slowly, rubbing his hands over his face. Maisie knew this was his way of calming himself down. He was afraid of the situation and doing his best to keep them together.

Maisie hated he had so much of this on his shoulders.

'We'll plan how we're going to keep in contact. How we're going to plan everything to get out of here. I know a couple of people who are willing to help us with that.'

'A couple of people?' Maisie sounded dubious about it. 'Everyone treats us badly because they're not the ones being abused. How are we going to trust anyone to help us?'

'Let's just say I know they're going to be loyal to us. You don't have to worry about any of that. I'll focus on that part.'

'That's easier said than done when everyone else has turned their backs on us.'

A name floated across Maisie's mind, which gave her pause. Nathan. Their old friend. She had thought about him occasionally, but the fact they hadn't been in contact with him for the last six years showed he had forgotten about them as well.

There was a chance he had been blocked from writing to them–they had been cut off from their father, after all–but Maisie didn't know. She just knew she had lost a friend.

Someone she had thought of as someone who would protect her from anything. He had promised that, after all. Nathan's sister and parents had been the same; they had looked after her and Noah with no arguments. If only they could live with them. Maisie knew that would have been an option. Then they wouldn't be in this mess.

As far as she was concerned, she and Noah were on their own. And they were going to be stuck if they didn't get out of this soon.

'All right.' She took a deep breath. 'What do you suggest, then? How are we going to get out of here?'

'It's going to take time and more planning, but it'll happen.' Noah placed his hands on Maisie's shoulders, stopping her pacing and making her turn towards him. 'Trust me, Maisie. I'm going to look after you. I promise.'

Maisie trusted him. He was the only one she could do that with. She would be on her own if she wasn't able to, so trust was immediate and absolute. She nodded, blinking back her tears.

'I trust you. And I know you'll get me out of this.'

'Absolutely.' Noah hugged her tightly. 'I'm not going anywhere without you. We're stuck together, and that will not change.'

That declaration was enough for Maisie to burst into tears. She sobbed quietly against his chest, feeling the tears fall.

* * *

1888

'Come along, you!' Aunt Lily snapped as Maisie hurried into the foyer. 'You said you would be ready ages ago.'

'Sorry, Aunt Lily. I had to make sure everything was packed onto the cart.' Maisie didn't look directly at the woman as she put her coat on. 'I don't want to forget anything.'

Aunt Lily grunted before turning away. Maisie was glad about that; she didn't want to have any further conversation with her aunt. The vegetables were loaded onto the cart, and she was going to be driving it into Buxton while her aunt went on ahead in her carriage.

It would be up to Maisie to sell everything on her own while Aunt Lily did some shopping. She would come by to make sure that Maisie was doing as she was told, but she wouldn't help. She was prepared to let Maisie flounder doing something she hated.

The market was important, and while Aunt Lily and Uncle Thomas had enough money that they didn't need to do anything like sell vegetables, they were happy getting whatever they could. And it humiliated Maisie into doing something she hated.

They got little from it anymore now that it was just her doing it. This indicated to Maisie that they were simply doing it to humiliate her and force her to live through something she hated doing.

That just made her hate them even more. She couldn't wait to get away from them.

And it would be today. After nine months of planning through letters and snatching moments with her brother, it was finally happening. Maisie and Noah were going to be running away. And their aunt and uncle weren't going to be able to do anything about it.

She just had to get to the market and pretend she was doing her job. Then Noah would find her, having run away from the quarry, and they would use the little they had managed to scrimp and save to get a carriage back to Derby. Once there, they had a few options, one of them being they found their father and begged for him to take them back. Maisie was concerned that he would refuse, though. Would he turn them away?

But there was the option of going into the workhouse. While Maisie knew neither of them wanted that, she knew it was preferable to the mess they had been living in. Those who ran those places would be better than Aunt Lily and Uncle Thomas.

It would be a relief to get away from them.

It didn't take long to get into Buxton. It was mid-March, and while it was still a little muddy underfoot it was nice weather. There were a few clouds in the sky, but not enough for Maisie to worry about getting rain. Aunt Lily had probably hoped there was rain so her niece would get soaked.

Maisie had often wondered if her aunt took joy in people's suffering. She certainly looked smug whenever Maisie was out in the cold and was shivering so hard her teeth were chattering.

No more of that.

They found their usual spot, and Maisie jumped down from the cart. Aunt Lily leaned out of the window and beckoned her niece over.

'I'm going to have some tea with a friend and do a bit of shopping,' she said curtly. 'You set up the stall and prepare everything.'

'Yes, Aunt Lily.'

'I want you to have sold at least a third of your wares by the time I get back. If you haven't, you're not going to get any dinner tonight.'

Maisie frowned, but she didn't say anything. Protesting would just make it worse, and she wanted to get rid of her aunt as soon as possible. 'Yes, Aunt Lily.'

Aunt Lily looked her up and down and a smile tugged at her mouth.

'You're growing into a proper young woman, Maisie. I'm pleased you're doing as you're told. You've come a long way since we last had to speak to you.'

Maisie didn't say anything. She wanted to, but she didn't want to cause any ire. This plan had to happen without any problems. 'I'll begin the setup now,' she said, giving her aunt a slight curtsy before turning away.

'Good girl. I'll be back in about two hours. Make sure the money profits are healthy by the time I return.'

Maisie didn't respond. She just concentrated on getting the vegetable boxes onto the stall, preparing for the onslaught of customers. It was not going to be as Aunt Lily expected when she got back. By that time, Maisie would be gone, and with the sight of free vegetables, people would have helped themselves to pretty much everything.

So, Aunt Lily would have lost a slave and her produce. Maisie couldn't think of anything better. It would serve her right.

As she put the boxes out, she heard the carriage being pulled away. Glancing over her shoulder, she watched Aunt Lily leaving, the older woman pulling up the shutter on the window with a snap. She didn't like people looking in and making comments, but Maisie didn't think she did herself any favours by looking out and openly sneering.

She couldn't believe that she was related to such a snob.

The carriage turned a corner in the street, and Maisie stopped what she was doing. She scanned the growing crowd, looking for Noah. He said he would be there once she arrived, and then they could head out. There was a carriage that travelled between Buxton and Derby, and they could catch it before it left for the day. It would take most of the day to get back, but it meant they would get away.

If Noah wasn't here, Maisie didn't know what she should do. Should she try to leave on her own? But how was she going to do it when she barely had any money? Aunt Lily had left the money box with her so they could store the money after selling vegetables, but Maisie was loath to take anything that would accuse her of being a thief.

'Maisie? Is that you?'

Maisie turned at the female voice. There was something about that voice that sounded familiar. A fair-haired woman a little taller than her in her twenties wearing a dove-grey dress was standing by the cart, staring at her with her mouth open. She looked as if she had seen a ghost.

'Oh, my God,' she gasped. 'It really is you. I didn't think I'd recognise you this long after the last time I saw you.'

Something clicked in Maisie's mind. She knew exactly who this woman was now. She stared at the young woman. 'Bethany? Bethany North?'

Bethany smiled. 'The very same. More or less.'

Maisie didn't know what to say for a moment. Her childhood friend's older sister was here in Buxton. She couldn't believe what she was seeing. Her immediate reaction was to jump on Bethany and hug her until she was sure this wasn't a dream.

'I…what…' She looked her up and down. 'I can't believe it. You're here?'

'I am.' Bethany moved towards her, giving her a smile as tears shimmered in her eyes. 'I can't believe you're here. When Nathan said you had been taken to live with your aunt, I didn't think we'd see you again. Now you're here…'

'What are you doing in Buxton?' Maisie asked. 'Have you moved here?'

'No, my husband and I were taking a few days here visiting his family. We're heading back to Derby today.'

'Husband?'

'Yes, I got married. Do you remember Christian Barker?'

'He's the son of your father's business partner, isn't he?'

'Yes.' Bethany blushed a little. 'We started courting when I was nineteen. We married not long after.'

Bethany got married? Maisie's heart swelled for her friend, only to squeeze when she realised she had missed it. She had been made into a slave for her aunt while her friends were moving on and growing up. She blinked back her own tears. This was not a time to cry.

'What are you doing here?' Bethany asked. 'Are you working the market?'

'I...'

That was when Maisie spied Noah. He was across the street, staring at her as he waited for her to finish whoever she was talking to. It was then Maisie realised Noah couldn't see Bethany with the cart in the way and beckoned him over.

'It's better if we explain it to you.'

'We?' Bethany frowned. 'Do you mean Noah is with you?'

'You can see for yourself.' Maisie turned to Noah as he rounded the cart. 'Noah?'

Noah started to speak, only to stop when he saw Bethany. His eyes practically bulged out of his head as he stared, to the point both Bethany and Maisie awkwardly laughed.

'You don't need to look at me like I'm something in a cage,' Bethany said jovially. 'I know I'm not that frightening to look at.'

'Oh. Right. Sorry.' Noah approached and embraced her. 'It's so good to see you again, Bethany. What are you doing here?'

'Visiting family. Now my husband and I are heading back to Derby today? He's joining me shortly.' Bethany peered at him before looking at Maisie. 'What on earth's happened to you two? You're looking thinner than you should, and you're covered in dust, Noah. What's happened to you since you left?'

Noah glanced at Maisie, and she knew what he was thinking.

They had a saviour here, and they should make the most of it. She nodded at him, which gave Noah the approval. They needed as much help as they could. Noah looked back at Bethany.

'It's a bit difficult to explain, but let's put it this way: we're running away. This was meant to be the day.'

Bethany's eyes widened. 'Running away? Why?'

'Can we explain to you later? If we're caught here, we'll never be able to leave.' Noah nodded at Maisie. 'Both of us need to get out of here. I know this is taking a liberty, but do you think you can help us? We just want to get back to Derby.'

'Of course. You don't need to ask.' Bethany looked around. 'My husband should be joining us with his carriage shortly. Then you can tell us what's going on.'

Maisie almost burst into tears hearing that. She swallowed back the hard lump in her throat. 'You would do that without question?' she croaked.

Bethany gave her a smile. 'You two practically grew up with me. I know that you're not the type to say you're running away without proper cause. And the sight of you is enough to make me concerned. I'll do whatever I can. Besides,' she added. 'Nathan would never forgive me if he heard about this.'

'Will we get to see Nathan as well?' Maisie asked before Noah could say anything.

'Absolutely. I'll make sure of it.' Bethany turned her head as a carriage entered the street. 'That's my husband. I need to tell him first, and then we can go.'

'Will he allow this?' Noah questioned.

Bethany snorted. 'He won't have a choice. I'm going to make sure you come back with me. If he doesn't like it, he can walk back to Derby.'

Maisie couldn't help but laugh at that remark. That was very much something Bethany would do.

'Anyway, come along.' Bethany beckoned them to follow her.

'The sooner we leave, the sooner we can get back to where you belong. And you're going to tell me everything.'

CHAPTER 6

Nathan looked forward to going home. The light was fading fast in his office when the doors opened, and Bethany charged in, almost knocking over one of the other clerks. Bethany barely appeared to notice, rushing straight over to Nathan's desk.

That surprised him more than anything. Bethany had never come into his offices before. The few times they had met up after work, she had waited outside. Nathan hadn't wanted his employer to get annoyed that his older sister was wandering around. She meant well, and she was a decent person, but there were times when she could get in the way.

Nothing much had changed since they were kids.

But there was something more with the way she came in. Bethany's eyes were wide, her cheeks flushed, and she was panting heavily. She must have run up the stairs to get to him. And yet…

Something was going on. Nathan put his pen down as his sister joined him. 'What's going on? Why are you up here, Bethany?'

'I found them.'

'Who? What are you talking about?'

'Noah and Maisie Skinner!' Bethany gasped, leaning on the desk as she got her breath back. 'I found them.'

Nathan sat up at the mere mention of their names. He hadn't heard anything from his friends since they left, and his letters to their aunt had gone unanswered. It had been years since he had heard anything about them. He stared at his sister. 'What? Did you say you found them?'

'Yes. They were in Buxton. I bumped into Maisie when Christian was getting the carriage.' Bethany's eyes sparkled. 'They came back with me. They're downstairs.'

That had Nathan shooting to his feet. Had he heard her correctly?

As if sensing his next question, Bethany nodded. 'Yes, that's right. They're downstairs in my carriage with Christian. And they want to see you.'

Nathan felt like he was in a strange dream. What was going on here? His friends were actually within reach?

'North!' His employer stuck his head out of his office, scowling at him across the room. 'Will you sit down and get back to your work? You've got too much to do there.'

'Sorry, Mr McDonald,' Nathan called back, grabbing his jacket and shrugging it on. 'I've just been told something important. I'll be right back, sir.'

'What's more important than doing your work?'

'I won't be long. I promise!'

Nathan hurried out of the room before Mr McDonald could say anything more. Hopefully, he wouldn't get into trouble for this, but right now, he didn't care. He just wanted to get down to his friends and see them again.

And demand a few explanations. Noah had promised they would keep in touch, that they wouldn't lose contact. But it had been six years and nothing. Nathan understood life happened and it would become harder to write back and forth, but this was Noah Skinner. He was not someone who broke a promise.

Hurrying down the stairs, almost tripping over his own feet, Nathan followed Bethany out to the carriage waiting in the street. Her husband Christian was by the open door, speaking to someone inside. He nodded at Nathan as he joined him.

'Take it easy. Both are quite fragile. They've been through a lot.'

'It's really Noah and Maisie?' Nathan asked. 'They're really here?'

'Nathan?'

Nathan heard the female voice and turned as a head stuck out of the carriage. She was older, and her features had changed a little, but there was no mistaking Maisie Skinner. Especially with those big eyes Nathan remembered.

He stared as she managed to get herself out of the carriage, holding onto Christian's arm as she wobbled. He was shocked at the sight of her. Maisie had to be fifteen now, but with her thin frame and short stature, she looked even younger. Her clothes were close to rags; they were practically hanging off her. Nathan couldn't believe what he was seeing. Maisie and Noah had meant to be with their aunt in Buxton, weren't they? What had happened for them to be like this?

'Maisie?'

Maisie gave him a timid smile, biting her lip as she hovered by Christian. 'It's me. It's been a long time, Nathan.'

Nathan didn't even think before he reacted. He reached for her and pulled her into a hug, trying not to clutch at her tightly in case she snapped in half. Maisie clung to him, burying her face against his chest as she began to sob. Nathan's heart broke hearing this, finding himself welling up as well.

This was not a reunion he had been expecting. Not at all.

'Nathan!'

Noah was now clambering out of the carriage, throwing himself onto Nathan as well. He almost knocked him and Maisie over, but Nathan caught him and hugged his friend just as fiercely. Noah looked as bad as his sister. He was tall, even taller than Nathan, but he was slim. There was some solid muscle on him, but he was bruised all over. There were also bruises on his face, looking as if he had been thrown around a lot.

He couldn't begin to describe the anger building in his stomach seeing his friends like this.

'I can't believe this.' Nathan managed to draw himself back to look at them, their pale faces staring back. 'What happened to you? Why did you vanish as you did?'

'We were lied to, Nathan,' Noah said grimly. 'Father didn't send us to Aunt Lily to live with her. He used us to pay off his debts.'

'What?'

'It's true,' Bethany said, moving to stand beside her husband. Their expressions were equally grim. 'Their aunt and uncle were keeping them as slaves in the house. Barely getting any pay but working at all hours of the day and night.'

'It's been like this for six years.' Maisie spoke through her tears, rubbing at her eyes with her sleeve. 'Father hasn't spoken to us, and we haven't been able to leave. We were going to run away, but then Bethany...she came upon us.'

'It's a good thing I did, too. When Christian and I were leaving with them, their aunt was coming the other way to an empty vegetable stall that was being taken apart by people wanting something for free. We didn't stay around to see what happened there.'

'Although I'm sure I heard her scream,' Maisie muttered. 'That terrified me. She has a temper. Both do.'

'They used to beat us,' Noah growled. 'They're always making us do the worst jobs, and then we're beaten for not doing as they wanted. When we were caught discussing running away and getting back to Father, we were separated. I was sent to work in the quarry, and Maisie was forced to work outside in any conditions without any reprieve.'

Nathan stared at Maisie. She was chewing at her bottom lip so hard he was surprised it wasn't bleeding. He wanted to pull her into his arms again, but then Bethany cleared her throat, drawing his attention away.

'We're going to take them back to the house, Nathan. You finish your work and come back as soon as you can.' Bethany took Maisie's hand and smiled. 'We were going to head straight home, but they wanted to see you first.'

Nathan wanted them to stay or to even go home with them. But Maisie and Noah looked exhausted, and he knew that what he wanted was not important. They were the priority. He took a deep breath.

'All right. I'll finish work. Then I'll come straight back.' He managed a smile at Maisie. 'I'll be home as soon as I can. You'll be safe with Bethany.'

'I know.' Maisie gave him a tremulous smile. 'Thank you, Nathan.'

Nathan couldn't believe what he was hearing or seeing right. It was scary that his friends were here in their state. How could anyone think what they went through was all right?

That aunt and uncle had to be insane.

* * *

MAISIE FELT a lot warmer after having a hot bath, a warm drink, and fresh clothes. Bethany had a few items that were a little big on Maisie, but they were better than the rags she had been wearing. She had struggled not to bring up her food again after wolfing it down, but she couldn't help herself. She was so hungry.

It felt like she was in a dream and going to wake up any

second now to find she was still in her bed back at Aunt Lily's house. Maisie was terrified that was going to happen.

But this was really happening. She was here in Bethany's house, along with her husband and children. According to Nathan's sister, it was close to his workplace, so he had moved in with them when their parents moved to the country.

It was a large, spacious townhouse, far bigger than the solitary home Aunt Lily and Uncle Thomas had lived in. And instead of coldness, there was warmth and happiness and the laughter of children. Maisie hadn't realised that Bethany had had children. Robyn was three, and Sarah had just turned one.

Then again, she had been away for a long time, so it was no surprise.

It was something Maisie missed. Laughter. She was glad to have it back, even if it wasn't hers.

As she curled up under a blanket on the window seat, watching people go by on the main street, she wondered what they were thinking, what they were doing. There was something beautiful about seeing what life was meant to be like.

Maisie wished she had fought her father about leaving home when she did. Then she might not be in this position.

'Maisie?'

Maisie's heart missed a beat when she heard Nathan's voice. Had he returned home already? He entered the room, looking as splendid as he had when she saw him outside his office earlier. He had grown a lot, almost as tall as Nathan, and he was well built. His jaw was more square, and he had a dusting of a beard across his jaw.

The cute boy she had known had grown into a very handsome young man. Maisie couldn't stop herself from staring at him. Especially when she remembered how strong his arms had felt around her earlier. She hadn't wanted to leave.

She shifted on the window seat and smiled. 'How was work?'

'Same as usual. Although I'm sure I've got a lot to do tomorrow. I had to rush to get back here.' Nathan regarded her thoughtfully. 'You look better than you did earlier. It's surprising what a hot bath and food will do for you.'

Maisie shrugged. 'I guess. I can't remember the last time I bathed like that. It was always with cold or tepid water, and we were given scraps.'

'That part I'm not surprised about, given how thin you are.' Nathan crossed the room and gestured at the window seat. 'Mind if I sit with you?'

'Of course not.'

Maisie shifted over to allow him to sit, curling her legs under her. They were very close now, and her heart was racing. If she stretched her feet out a little, she would end up touching him. Maisie's mouth went dry at the thought.

What was wrong with her? 'Have you seen Noah?' she asked. 'I don't know where he is…'

'Not yet. I wanted to see you first.'

'Me?'

Nathan's cheeks went a little pink, and he cleared his throat. 'Well, you were the first one I came across, so I thought I'd see you before I went looking for him. At least you're looking a little better.' He leaned back against the window and looked her over. 'Six years. You've really grown up.'

'So have you,' Maisie replied. 'Bethany told me you're working to become a solicitor.'

'I'm still in training. I'm currently one of the clerks at a law firm. But I'm going to be qualified soon.'

'And your parents are well, right?'

Nathan nodded, his expression softening. 'Yes, they're well. They're living in Kent now and making the most of the quiet with regular trips into Canterbury. They're going to be delighted when they hear about you. I know Mother missed you two, especially.'

Maisie swallowed. 'It seems like your family missed us, but

when it came to our actual family...they treated us like we were nothing.'

Nathan's jaw tightened. His eyes were still the same colour that snagged Maisie's attention when they first met. She couldn't look away now.

Some things never changed.

'I can't begin to imagine the pain and horrors you went through with those people, and I don't want you to go through it again.' Nathan's tone was gentle, and his expression was compassionate, with his full attention on Maisie. 'You and Noah don't have to go back.'

'We're never going back,' Maisie said immediately. 'It doesn't matter about the debt. Neither Noah nor I will go back to that woman and her husband.'

'What about your father?'

'I don't know what to think. He never reached out to us, and I don't know if he's still alive.' Maisie scowled. 'I'm kind of hoping he is dead because that would serve him right. Is that too much?'

'Given what you've been through, I'm not really surprised.' Nathan reached out after a moment and took her hand as it poked out of the blanket. 'I've spoken to Bethany and Christian. They said they have plenty of room for the two of you to stay with us.'

'Bethany said something about that.' Maisie licked her lips, aware of how warm his hand was around her fingers. 'Noah said we could work for her, do whatever we can to repay her kindness.'

Nathan looked surprised. 'You want to work for them?'

'We know how to work in a household, and it would feel like charity if we stayed here without doing anything. We might as well make the most of what we've been taught.'

'Are you sure about that?'

Maisie nodded. 'It's only fair. If you want to treat us like family, we're not going to argue. But we want to be able to earn what we can, too.'

Nathan was silent for a moment. Then he smiled and squeezed her fingers. 'It's going to be all right, Maisie. We'll look after you. You don't have to worry about anything else again.'

Maisie was going to hold him to that. She wanted to trust that he was right. Because she had no intention of going back to what her life had been before.

CHAPTER 7

1895

'I'm just going to see Beatrice,' Noah said.

Maisie looked up and saw Noah standing at the edge of the garden. She sat back on her haunches and smiled. 'That's the third time this week you've been to see her,' she pointed out.

'What's wrong with that?' Noah shrugged. 'We're courting, aren't we? There's nothing wrong with visiting her.'

'You're meant to be working. So is she. It's not your afternoon off.' Maisie gestured towards the house. 'If Bethany and Christian find out what you've been up to, they're going to get really annoyed.'

Noah grinned. Maisie groaned. She could tell that her brother wasn't too bothered about that. He had met a young woman who found him attractive and wanted to be around him whenever she could, but it was more than a little annoying that Noah would neglect his work just to see her. Maisie could understand young love, although she disapproved of what her older brother was doing.

'You're approaching thirty in a few years, Noah.' She got up and walked around the edge of the vegetable garden towards him, dusting the soil off her dress. 'Aren't you a little old to be behaving like a lovesick fool?'

'I'm not lovesick!'

'What do you call sneaking over to see a girl you can't bear to be away from for more than a few minutes? Beatrice is a sweet girl, but you need to calm down; otherwise, both of you could get into trouble.' Maisie glanced towards the house again. 'Despite Bethany knowing us and taking us in, she can dismiss you for not doing your work. Then what do you think will happen there?'

'She won't dismiss us. She would appreciate me finding love and keeping it.' Noah winked. 'She's soft-hearted like that.'

'Don't push your luck.' Maisie sighed and shook her head. 'Honestly, Noah, you really need to get your priorities straight. It's going to get you into trouble one day.'

'Oh, I've got my priorities. Maybe you should do the same.' Noah reached out and tickled her chin, which made Maisie slap his hand away. 'It doesn't do you good to be working so hard all the time.'

'I don't mind.'

'Change your priorities, and then you might find some joy in life.'

Maisie frowned. 'You think I don't have any joy? I have time to myself.'

'Oh, really? I don't know about that.'

This was a regular argument. Maisie did whatever she could to keep herself busy, and she felt like she was being fulfilled. Far different to how things had been for them years ago where she was being worked to the bone. She just enjoyed working for Bethany's family. Things were so much better.

She was glad they had managed to run away, to get away from her aunt and uncle. It felt like a bizarre dream that could have happened to them. Yet here they were, several years on, working for their friends.

It was certainly preferable. Maisie didn't want to ruin that.

'Maybe you should ask Nathan to take you out somewhere,' Noah said slyly.

Maisie started. 'What are you saying? Why would you suggest that?'

'Oh, I don't know. Maybe because I know that would make you smile.' Noah chuckled as Maisie's mouth fell open. 'I'm not blind, Maisie. I know you find my friend attractive. It's not that hard to notice when you're around.'

Maisie could feel her face getting warm, and it had nothing to do with the heat from the sun. Noah's smile widened, his expression smug. Maisie tried to recover herself, but it didn't work very well. She was still spluttering when she tried to talk.

'But…no…what are you talking about? He's just a friend who's helped us out, Noah!'

'And? Since when did that get in the way?'

'And in case it's slipped your mind, big brother, he's the brother of our employer,' Maisie reminded him. 'Bethany might be a family friend, but there is a social hierarchy. I can't have anything to do with Nathan because of my status.'

'Do you think he cares about that?'

'What are you talking about?'

'Talk to him next time you see him and pay attention to how closely he's listening. I think you'll understand, eventually.' Noah turned away. 'I'd better go before I get caught. Good thing Beatrice is only across the street, or I'd be in serious trouble sneaking away.'

'You're going to get into serious trouble if you do anyway,' Maisie called after him. 'Noah!'

But her brother simply waved a hand over his shoulder as he walked off. Groaning, Maisie shook her head and turned away. That man was going to get them both into trouble if he wasn't careful. Maisie wasn't interested in keeping her brother safe when it meant dragging her into the mess he was creating. But

Noah was still family; it was hard to forget that. Maisie loved him, even if he drove her mad.

At least he was finding a fresh start and love for himself. After years of being abused by their aunt, it was nice to have something of their own, something fresh and new that made them feel better about their lives. Noah had fallen in love and Maisie…

She was happy. She didn't think she would be able to say that, but she was. Being a maid wasn't the best job, yet it was a very worthwhile one. Plus, she was with Bethany and her lovely family, including Nathan.

He still lived with his sister as it was close to his workplace, which had had a change of management lately. Nathan had worked hard over the years and qualified to become a solicitor. Now he was a junior partner in the law firm he started at years ago. Maisie couldn't be any more proud of him.

She had told him that many times, and her friend had blushed. He had been doing that a lot lately during their time in the evenings together. Maisie would work while Nathan was in the same room. Sometimes, Bethany caught them sitting and talking, but she said nothing. It was like she was aware of something happening.

Was there something going on? Maisie knew she was in love with Nathan, that was without a doubt. She had figured out her feelings for him years ago, but she was never going to act on them. How could she? They were of different classes now. Nathan was a successful young solicitor, while Maisie…

She was simply a maid. No lawyer was going to lower himself to her level. It was painful to know, but Maisie was confident it wouldn't change. She didn't believe they could forget all of that and end up together, even if her thoughts wanted it to happen. She knew her place, though, and she wasn't about to cause any upset for anyone.

It was a shame, but Maisie could cope with it. Just about.

'Maisie!'

Cook was calling for her. Maisie turned and saw the stout woman walking towards her along the garden path, her stride quick and firm. There was someone behind her, but they were mostly obscured by Cook.

Checking that Noah was out of sight, and she wasn't going to get into trouble for covering for him–albeit reluctantly–Maisie dusted herself down and approached the older woman.

'Yes, Cook? Is there something I can do?'

'We've got a new kitchen maid today. Mrs Barker wanted her to start as soon as possible, seeing as we're getting a little behind.' Cook turned to the woman behind her. 'This is Charlotte. Charlotte, this is Maisie.'

Maisie froze as soon as she saw the woman. There was no mistaking her. It had been years since they last saw each other, but Maisie would never forget the beady dark eyes, the sneering mouth, and the thin frame that made her look taller than she already was. Right now, she was smirking at Maisie as if she had done something incredible.

Aunt Lily's maid was here, standing right in front of her.

Maisie could feel her chest tightening, and she struggled to breathe. Things started to sway, and Maisie didn't realise that she had stumbled until Cook caught her.

'Oh, goodness, Maisie! What's the matter with you?'

'I…I don't know.' Maisie managed to get her footing again and straightened up. 'I'm sorry, Cook. I think it's a bit warm out here.'

'Well, it's a good thing that Charlotte's here. She's going to be helping now, so she can do the garden while you can recover.'

Charlotte looked a bit put out by that, but Maisie was trying not to look at her. She could feel a knot forming in her stomach. There was no chance of this being a coincidence, not when Charlotte was incredibly loyal to Aunt Lily. She had to be at the Barker house for a reason.

Fear gripped her. Did Aunt Lily know where Maisie and

Noah were? After all this time, had they had managed to find them?

'You'd better sit down, Maisie,' Charlotte said, her tone sounding concerned but her expression saying otherwise. 'You're looking incredibly pale.'

'I think that's a good idea.' Cook moved Maisie to a nearby bench and urged her to sit. 'I'll get you a glass of water. Just take a moment. Charlotte, stay with her in case she faints.'

Maisie didn't want the cook to leave. She didn't want to be alone with Charlotte. The woman was smirking at her more freely now, sharing a secret with herself. Maisie's chest was tightening more, and she couldn't get the air in. She pressed a hand to her chest, and Cook patted her shoulder.

'It'll be fine, dear. I won't be long.'

Then she hurried off, leaving Charlotte and Maisie alone. Charlotte stood over Maisie, arms folded with a smirk on her face.

'I never thought I'd see you again. Not after you two ran away.'

'What are you doing here, Charlotte?' Maisie demanded. 'You would never leave Aunt Lily's household.'

'How do you know?'

'Because you're far too loyal to her. You would do whatever she said to get what your mistress wanted.'

Charlotte laughed. It wasn't a very nice sound. 'It's good to know that you've grown up with a brain. Of course I would never leave my mistress. She's been very good to me.'

'Well, if you don't mind me saying so, I had a very different experience with her.' Maisie tried to draw in air, but it didn't work. 'You're here for a reason, aren't you? And it's not for a new position.'

Charlotte leaned in, and Maisie tried to draw back, but she was up against the wall of the house and couldn't go far. Charlotte's face was inches from hers, the sneer making Maisie whimper. Even after all these years, and being a grown woman, she was still scared of the lady before her. Charlotte had been a cruel, vindictive woman who would do anything for her mistress. It was why she and Aunt Lily had gotten along so well. They were just perfect for each other.

The fact she was here had to mean Aunt Lily knew where Maisie and Noah were. There couldn't be any other reason for her being here.

'Your aunt has been very worried about you. She's been looking for you for years now.'

'You're lying,' Maisie said faintly. 'She's not been worried.'

'Oh, she has.' Charlotte's eyes drifted over her face, and Maisie couldn't help but shiver. 'You could tell anyone about what happened to you. She isn't about to let the two of you say anything against her and her husband. Imagine what she's going to say when she finds out you're only a stone's throw away from where she lives.'

'You've been looking for us all this time?'

Charlotte's mouth curved. 'You've got a debt to pay off, haven't you? You need to pay it.'

'We were with your mistress for six years,' Maisie shot back. 'We should have paid it back by that point. We were free to go.'

'Not until your mistress says so.'

'Maisie?'

Maisie almost burst into tears at the sound of the familiar voice. Charlotte pulled back abruptly as Nathan came around the corner. Her heart pounded when she saw him, her mouth going dry. Every time she saw Nathan, it was the same reaction. Maisie couldn't stop herself from staring at her friend. He had grown into a very handsome man, tall and broad-shouldered with a muscular build and a smile that made his eyes twinkle. Maisie's knees went weak at the sight of him, and she felt like a fool stumbling over her words.

Now, he was like the most comforting sight she had ever seen.

'Nathan.' She shot to her feet. 'What are you doing back?'

'I came home for lunch.' Nathan peered at her curiously before glancing at Charlotte. 'What's happened? Cook said you'd come over faint.'

'I…I'm fine.' Maisie didn't look at Charlotte, gesturing up at the sky. 'It's just a warm day, that's all.'

Nathan's expression said he wasn't convinced. He was watching Charlotte, who was standing with her shoulders back, hands clasped before her, giving Maisie a slight smile that looked very smug.

'And you are?' he asked sharply.

'I'm Charlotte.' Charlotte dropped a quick curtsy. 'I'm the new kitchen maid.'

'Right.' Nathan beckoned Maisie to join him. 'Come on, Maisie. Let's get you inside. I think the sun is getting too much for you.'

Maisie didn't need to be told twice. She practically ran to him, almost flinging her arm around his waist as she joined him. Nathan put his arms around her shoulders and led her away.

'What's wrong?' he murmured. 'You're shaking.'

'Get me away from her.' Maisie's voice trembled. She resisted the urge to look over her shoulder. 'I'll tell you, but get me away from her.'

She was shocked at the fact Charlotte managed to get past the family and into the household. Something had to have gone wrong somewhere. Now, Maisie felt like she was panicking again.

* * *

NATHAN WAS CONFUSED at Maisie's reaction. She had turned into a warm, vibrant young woman who had blossomed and loved her work. To see her panicking and looking like she was about to collapse with a strange woman standing over her was a shock. And she was terrified; he could tell that much.

He wanted to put his arms around her and hold her close until she stopped shaking, but he didn't. That would mean he wouldn't be able to let go.

Steering Maisie through the house, he led her into Christian's study. His brother-in-law wouldn't mind, not if he knew the circumstances. He and Bethany were considerate of all of their servants, especially Maisie and Noah. Shutting the door behind him, Nathan led Maisie to a nearby chair and urged her to sit down.

'Maisie, talk to me.' Nathan crouched before her and took her hands. 'What happened? I've not seen you like that for a long time.'

'I…' Maisie audibly swallowed before licking her lips. 'I don't know what to do, Nathan. I'm terrified.'

'Terrified of what?'

'Charlotte.'

Nathan frowned. 'The new maid. What's wrong with her?'

But Maisie was shaking her head vigorously. Her hands shook in his grip, and Nathan realised she was clenching her fists. He was shocked at her reaction.

'She's not new. That's Aunt Lily's maid.'

'What?'

'Charlotte works for Aunt Lily. She's loyal to that woman alone. And, from what she said, they've been looking for Noah and me for years.' Maisie was breathing fast and heavy. 'Now they've found out, and we need to go back and finish paying off the debt.'

Nathan couldn't believe what he was hearing. Maisie and Noah had told him all about the things that had happened with their aunt and uncle up in Buxton, and how they had been mistreated. He had been shocked by what they went through, all to pay off their father's debts.

No child should have to go through that, and they certainly shouldn't have to be treated so badly by their own relatives. It was terrifying that nobody had helped them despite seeing the treatment over the years. It knotted his stomach to know his friends had been subjected to such cruelty.

Now, Maisie seemed to have turned into that scared little girl again.

He drew her into his arms, urging Maisie to rest her head on his shoulder. She let out a little sob, but she didn't pull away. Nathan rubbed her back, waiting for her to calm down. He didn't know what to say. Seeing her like this was scary to him. Maisie was a strong woman, and Nathan had always admired that. This was a state he felt nervous about.

It made him feel helpless.

'I can't believe they're still looking for us,' Maisie croaked, finally lifting her head and sitting up. 'I would have thought they would have given up years ago. It seems extreme to try to chase after two children who ran away, and that they clearly didn't want around.'

'There is that debt,' Nathan reminded her. 'If they had that agreement with your father…'

'He would never have allowed us to be like that,' Maisie protested. 'He wasn't good with money, and he might not have shown it much, but he loved us. He wouldn't have agreed to send us to Aunt Lily's if he knew we were going to be treated badly.'

'But he agreed to send you there to pay off his debts,' Nathan pointed out. He sat back on his haunches. 'I think as long as he paid off what he owed, he didn't care what happened to you.'

Maisie flinched, and she looked close to tears again. Nathan didn't want to be cruel about it, but he was certain that Charles Skinner had done exactly that. He had been a gambler who loved to use money for that more than he cared to admit. It was terrifying that he could behave in such a manner and use his children for his own means. Nathan had a few choice words to say to Charles when he finally saw him.

'I think we should have been released from all of that years ago,' Maisie said, wiping at her eyes with the heel of her hands. 'We must have paid it all off. He can't have had a debt that big it ended up taking six years to pay off.'

Nathan fumbled in his pocket and found his handkerchief. Then he took Maisie's hand and pressed the cloth into it. Maisie faltered, glancing at him before looking down at the handkerchief. Her fingers were warm and soft against his, and Nathan had to stop himself from holding onto her for longer. Biting her lip, Maisie pulled her hand back slowly, giving Nathan a tiny smile.

'Thank you.'

'You don't ever need to thank me. You know I'll always help you.'

Nathan stood and began to pace, although he paused by the window. Christian's study looked out into the garden, and there was a clear view of the vegetable garden. Charlotte was there, finishing Maisie's job with a scowl and clearly not looking happy. She even kicked the basket at one point and knocked it over, scattering the vegetables across the path. Nathan watched as she stood there, hands on her hips, with her annoyed expression tilted back to the sun. With a slump of her shoulders, she picked everything up.

What were Bethany and Christian thinking, hiring her like this? They had to know about Charlotte and what she had done before. Or maybe they didn't. It had been seven years since Maisie and Nathan came to work for them. That was enough time to have passed for someone to believe they were safe enough.

Maisie hadn't forgotten, though. Nathan needed to speak to his sister. They couldn't have Charlotte present when she was a clear threat.

'I don't know what to do,' Maisie said quietly, a slight crack in her voice. 'I can't work with her around. I'm going to be on edge all the time, especially when I know Aunt Lily is still looking for us.'

Nathan turned to her. 'I don't know what my sister was thinking,' he said gruffly.

'She probably didn't realise. It's not as if she saw what Charlotte looked like. And Charlotte is certainly not going to admit she knew me from before.' Maisie was twisting the handkerchief in her hands now. 'I don't know what to do. I'm scared, Nathan. Noah and I must have paid that debt off, so why would they want us back? I know Aunt Lily wouldn't want the two of us under her roof for longer than necessary.'

'Either the debt was far bigger than anyone anticipated, or something more sinister is going on,' Nathan replied.

'Like what?'

'I don't know yet. We're going to have to figure it out.' Nathan watched as she put a knot into the handkerchief. She was going to tear it apart if she wasn't careful. 'Bethany and Christian will be back tomorrow. I'll talk to them then about if we can dismiss Charlotte.'

Maisie stared at him with wide eyes. 'But what about today? I can't work with her in the house. I'm going to be a nervous wreck. And what about when Noah comes back? He's going to see Charlotte, and he's going to be furious.'

'I'm aware of that.' Nathan rubbed his hands over his face. 'Look, they're only on the other side of London. It's not like they're on the other side of the country. I'll send a letter right now and ask for Bethany to return.'

'Are you sure?'

'You want Charlotte gone, don't you? I don't have the authority to throw her out as I'm not her employer. Much as I would want to, but Bethany and Christian both told me to leave the household servants to them, and they'll deal with it.' Nathan had been agreeable at the time, but now he wished he didn't have that rule. 'My sister will come as soon as she knows the truth. She won't let anything happen to you.'

Maisie was still trembling. She lowered her head, and Nathan heard her starting to cry. His heart cracking, he went to her.

'Oh, Maisie. Please don't cry. It's going to be fine.'

'I'm so scared, Nathan,' Maisie croaked, rubbing the handkerchief over her face. 'I'm just terrified Charlotte's going to do something. What if Aunt Lily comes here? What if she tries to take Noah and me back? I…I can't…'

She pressed the handkerchief to her face and began to sob. Nathan didn't know what to do. He was not good at comforting someone when they were in distress. But this was Maisie, and he couldn't just stand there.

Pulling up another chair, he sat beside her and urged her to lean into him. Maisie went without any complaints, sobbing into his shoulder. Her whole body was shaking, and it didn't ease as Nathan rubbed her back, rocking her gently. It made Nathan feel useless, knowing that the woman he had fallen for was in such fear of her life.

He couldn't allow her to feel like that anymore. When they were reunited, Nathan had made a promise to look after her, that he would never let any harm come to her. And now he felt like he had failed.

CHAPTER 8

Maisie spent the rest of the day feeling nervous. She jumped at the slightest noise, and she could hardly concentrate. God only knew how many mistakes she made, aware that Charlotte was close by. She couldn't even go into the kitchen anymore, not when she knew the woman was there smirking at her. And Charlotte knew she was causing her discomfort. It was clear from the look on her face that she was aware and enjoying it.

Noah had found out shortly after returning from seeing Beatrice. As soon as he caught sight of Charlotte, he tried to attack her. It was only when Nathan pulled him back and out of the room that he was able to calm down. Maisie was terrified that Noah might lose his position after attempting to assault Charlotte, but Nathan had assured her they wouldn't have anything to worry about.

Once Bethany returned, Charlotte was gone. Nathan had promised them that. His sister wouldn't allow her childhood friends to be in a position where they were uncomfortable. And once she heard about the situation, she would be furious. Although Maisie was surprised at how Charlotte had managed to get a job when Bethany was the one who hired the household staff.

But it wasn't like Charlotte was going to admit the truth when she was interviewing for the position. And Bethany had never met the woman in person, so Maisie could give her some grace. Her employer would make it right.

Bethany would never allow Noah and Maisie to be tormented by their past like this. Not willingly, anyway.

Noah was still angry about Charlotte being around, so Nathan had to have him close by to keep an eye on him. Maisie was worried about her brother. He had clearly shown his distaste for their aunt's maid, and Charlotte would now be on her guard. She would use it to her advantage if she got the chance.

This made Maisie glad that they were in the employ of old friends. Anyone else would have dismissed Noah immediately without checking the situation first.

A letter came early afternoon, and Maisie took it to Nathan, who was in his brother-in-law's study. Noah was there, standing by the window and scowling out into the garden. He barely turned as Maisie entered and approached Nathan. He looked up, and Maisie's heart missed a beat as his eyes met hers.

She really needed to stop; otherwise, she would make a fool of herself.

'This just arrived.' She held out the letter. 'Is it from Bethany?'

'Let's see.' Nathan took the letter, their fingers brushing for a moment in a way that made Maisie bite back a gasp, and he opened it. He nodded. 'Yes, it's from her. To say she's shocked is an understatement. She's on her way back right now. Christian will stay with his family and the children, but Bethany will be back shortly.'

Maisie almost sagged in relief. Thank goodness for that. If the letter had just arrived, it would mean Bethany wouldn't be far behind. Although Maisie was surprised she had written before leaving instead of returning immediately.

'Does she say anything else?' she asked.

'Just that we need to keep Charlotte to the kitchens, and she's not allowed in the rest of the house. I'll notify Cook about that.' Nathan stood up and gave Maisie a reassuring smile. 'We'll get this sorted, Maisie. I promise.'

Noah snorted. 'If you two had done your checks properly, then this wouldn't have happened.'

'It's not Nathan's fault,' Maisie pointed out.

'But someone should have found something out.' Noah's shoulders were tense and hunched, his arms folded as he glared out of the window. 'Of all the people to come here, why did it have to be her?'

Maisie didn't know what to say to that. She glanced at Nathan, who nodded.

'You go and carry on with your work. I'll keep Noah in here so he doesn't do anything stupid.'

'Nice to know you don't trust me,' Noah muttered.

Nathan pressed his fingers to the bridge of his nose. 'Even if Bethany and Christian are on your side, you can't attack a woman, Noah. You would have that following you around. It doesn't matter what she did to you; that will be what people remember. Especially when you've got someone as nasty as your aunt looking for you: she will make sure you have a ruined reputation. If you were dismissed from here, you'd be lucky to get another position without this coming back to bite.'

Noah glowered at him, his scowl practically etched into your face. 'There are times when I want you to be quiet,' he growled before turning away.

Maisie wanted to go to him and offer some comfort, but Nathan walked around the desk and placed a hand on her back. The sensation of the warm hand against her body made her jump.

'Leave him,' he whispered, steering her towards the door. 'I'll look after him. He'll be fine with me.'

'Are you sure?'

Nathan smiled. 'Do you trust me?'

There was never any doubt about that. Maisie nodded, and she saw something pass behind Nathan's eyes. He reached up and brushed his fingers across her jaw. Maisie wanted to lean into him and feel his touch even more, but she stopped herself. Now was not the time to be inappropriate, especially in front of her brother.

'I'll take care of Noah. You don't have anything to worry about.'

Maisie believed him, although a nagging sensation at the back of her mind was worried things were not going to be as simple as dismissing Charlotte. She was not going to leave easily, especially if Aunt Lily was determined to get her niece and nephew back. Even after all this time, she still wanted them around despite showing her clear distaste for them.

Either the debt had been a lot bigger than anyone thought, or there was something else going on.

Deciding that hovering around Nathan wasn't going to help, Maisie focused on her chores. She had quite a bit to do, and she needed her complete focus. If she didn't hurry up, she was going to end up working late into the night. Housework wasn't that difficult once she had a routine for it, and they were completed in a certain order, but there were times when Maisie wished it went a little faster.

She went upstairs and began to strip the beds. They were due to be changed, and the sheets needed to be washed. It wouldn't take long to change everything around, put the dirty sheets into the laundry room to be cleaned later, and then make the rooms presentable. The new sheets would be ready for Bethany once she returned.

It had felt odd working for someone she had known as a child in the beginning, but Bethany and Christian had made her feel welcome and were patient with her. Their children were adorable as well, and Maisie felt as if she belonged for the first time in years. It certainly helped that Nathan was present; he lit up the room for her whenever he walked in.

Maisie knew her feelings for Nathan needed to disappear, but that was easier said than done. They had always been there; she was sure of it. Then, being around him so much wasn't helping the situation. Even when she knew his presence was not making things better, Maisie couldn't bring herself to look for another position. She wanted to stay, even if it meant seeing Nathan and being unable to do anything about it.

Aunt Lily had called her a fool many times. There was a part of Maisie that suspected her aunt was right.

Pushing that out of her mind, Maisie concentrated on getting the beds in Bethany and Nathan's rooms stripped. She would change the sheets once everything was in the laundry room. Careful not to trip over her feet, she went to the stairs and started to make her way down, turning a little so she could see her feet securely placed on each step.

A sudden shove in her back startled her, and Maisie couldn't catch her balance before she tilted forwards. She was aware of a scream coming from her as she tumbled, the world spinning as her body hit the stairs, halting when she got to the bottom. The sheets had tangled themselves around her, and one had managed to go over her head.

Everything hurt. Things were spinning, and Maisie could feel pain everywhere on her body. She felt sick. Her head was pounding, and she couldn't move. She lay there, trying to get her bearings.

'Maisie!'

Someone began tugging at the sheets, pulling them away from her face. Then a blurred face appeared above her, hands gently brushing her hair away from her face.

'Maisie, look at me!' Hands cupped her head. 'Please, just look at me!'

It took a moment more for her vision to clear, but then Maisie saw Nathan leaning over her. The welcoming sight of him made her want to burst into tears again.

'Thank God!' He kissed her forehead. 'I thought you were...'

'I...what...'

Maisie looked up the stairs and saw Charlotte at the top. She just looked at her, her expression blank, before disappearing. Maisie tried to get up, only for Noah to appear beside her and Nathan, resting a hand on her shoulder.

'Don't try to get up, Maisie,' he urged. 'You've had a nasty tumble.'

'I didn't trip,' Maisie whispered. 'I...I was pushed.'

Noah and Nathan glanced at each other. Did they not believe her? Maisie lifted her arm, surprised that she was able to move it, and pointed up the stairs.

'I...it was Charlotte. I...I saw...her...'

Noah's jaw tightened. 'I'm going to kill her,' he growled, and then he charged up the stairs.

'Noah...' Nathan shouted after him. 'Get back here!'

But Noah didn't answer, disappearing on the landing. Just as he did, the front door opened, and Maisie was aware of footsteps. Then she heard a familiar gasp.

'Goodness! Nathan, what's happened to Maisie?'

'Your new maid,' Nathan said grimly. 'She pushed Maisie down the stairs.'

'What?' Bethany gasped. 'She did this?'

'Can you stay with her, Bethany? I need to make sure Noah doesn't do anything stupid.' Nathan looked at Maisie, his face still swimming in and out of focus. 'I'll be right back,' he promised. 'Bethany will look after you.'

'Nathan...'

'I promise you'll be fine.' He kissed her forehead again. 'Just lie still. We'll get this sorted.'

Then he stood up, easing Maisie back onto the floor, and

hurried up the stairs. A moment later, Bethany was leaning over her, her expression worried as she brushed Maisie's hair away from her face.

'Oh, Maisie,' she whispered. 'I can't believe this happened. I'm so sorry.'

Maisie almost asked what she was sorry about, but then she guessed. Bethany would have hired Charlotte and brought her into the house. If she wasn't to know, though…

'It's…not your fault…' She gulped.

Bethany snorted. 'Trust me, it is. I should never have taken her word. But that's going to be sorted now. She's gone, that much I can say.'

Maisie believed that. She was certain this would happen, but she didn't think it would be over. Now Charlotte was aware of where she was, Aunt Lily would be aware as well. If they really wanted her and Noah back, they would be determined to do so.

That part she wasn't looking forward to. If anything, it left her terrified.

* * *

'I CAN'T BELIEVE I hired that woman,' Bethany said for the fifth time as she and Nathan made their way through the streets, dodging past people going the other way in groups, barely acknowledging them. 'I brought her into the house.'

'You weren't to know,' Nathan assured her.

'But if I had known…'

'Bethany, how were you to know? She wasn't exactly going to tell you that she worked for the abusive woman who kept her niece and nephew prisoner for six years, was she? She knew what she was doing.'

Bethany still didn't look convinced. Nathan knew she was upsetting herself over the fact she had let one of her friend's abusers into the house. It was not something she would have done willingly. But they had caught it quickly, and Charlotte was already gone.

She had protested, but when Nathan said they would get the police to escort her out and tell them all about what Aunt Lily had done, that had made her scarper quickly. Nathan was glad that was sorted, although Maisie was still hurt.

The doctor had been sent for and checked her over, saying she had knocked her head, but there was nothing broken. He recommended plenty of rest, which Bethany had agreed to immediately. Maisie hadn't wanted to, but everyone urged her to lie down and sleep. Noah promised to stay with her, which made Nathan feel a little better. His friend wouldn't let his sister come to any harm.

Although he didn't see Charlotte breaking back in to try to get Maisie back. That would be ridiculous.

'I hope we find him,' Bethany remarked as they turned the corner. 'Do you think he's still here?'

'Charles Skinner is a man of habit. He wouldn't move on from what he knows and is comfortable with.'

'I would have thought you'd come looking for him long before this. I'm surprised you didn't.'

'Because Noah and Maisie didn't want to know. They were angry with him, and I knew bringing him to them before they were ready was going to make things worse.' Nathan shrugged. 'I'm just waiting for them to say they want to talk to him, that's all.'

'Hmm.' Bethany didn't look convinced. She peered up at her younger brother with an expression Nathan couldn't read properly. 'You'd do anything for Maisie, wouldn't you?'

Nathan blinked. 'Why would you say that?'

'Because you've always done everything for her. Even when we were children. You looked after her more than Noah did, and he's her brother.'

'I don't know what…'

'I've seen the way you are around her, Nathan,' Bethany went on. 'How you behave with her. It's like she's the only one in the room. And from the way she reacts whenever you're around, she shares your feelings.'

Nathan stared at his sister, unaware of people moving around them, until someone bumped into him and muttered something under their breath. He cleared his throat and moved aside, trying to keep out of the way of everyone leaving the area to head home. Nobody wanted to be around as soon as they had finished work.

'I...what...' Nathan stammered and shook himself. 'What are you talking about?'

Bethany sighed. 'Honestly, Nathan, you're really a fool at times, do you know that? Even Christian's noticed how Maisie behaves around you, and he's more oblivious than you are. Surely, you must have realised that you and she...'

'No, I haven't.'

'Then you really need to pay attention to it.' His sister folded his arms and shook her head. 'Honestly, Nathan, you've been pining after her for years. To the point you've refused to entertain another woman for courtship, and it's been driving our parents mad. You think they would disapprove of her, don't you?'

Nathan wanted to protest, but he knew she was right. His shoulders slumped. 'How can it work, Beth? I'm a solicitor; she's a maid. That social class difference is going to raise a lot of eyebrows, even with my parents. I don't want to hurt her like that.'

'It's more about hurting Maisie and less about the social differences?'

'Of course! I would marry her tomorrow if possible. But I don't want her to have people whispering in corners, wondering what she's been doing.' Nathan rubbed his hands over his face. 'She's been through a lot in her life. She doesn't deserve that.'

'Well, I'm sure the rumours will die down. It's not going to hurt or affect anyone, and if anyone has a problem, then they can just go away.' Bethany smiled. 'If it makes you feel any better, Mother and Father would approve.'

'Really?'

'They like Maisie. I heard Mother commenting about how sweet the two of you were at Christmas. I don't think either of them will be surprised if they find out you two are together.'

Nathan was thrown. His parents were aware of it? He had been careful not to say anything about his feelings for Maisie all this time. Had he been that obvious?

'Anyway, come on.' Bethany took his arm and got him moving again. 'We've got to go and find Charles Skinner. He's got a lot to answer for. Once we've dealt with his mess, you can talk to Maisie about whatever you want.'

Nathan wasn't about to argue with that. He just needed to get his focus back again; Bethany threw him off-guard. His sister was wonderful at that.

They reached the factory Charles had worked at before. Nathan wondered if they would find him. It had been fourteen years now since he sent his children away and cut contact with their family. He could have moved on elsewhere, or he might have died. But there had to be someone who knew where he was.

They could but try.

A tall, thin man with white hair stepped out of the door, blinking in the bright sunlight as he put his hat on. It took a moment, but Nathan recognised him. Even with the weight loss, there was no denying it was Charles Skinner.

His heart skipped a beat. Was this really happening? Nodding at Bethany, who appeared to have seen the same thing from her stunned expression, Nathan approached the older man.

'Mr Skinner?'

'That's me.' He peered at Nathan curiously. 'I know you, don't I? I can't place your face, though.'

'I'm Nathan North. I'm a friend of Noah and Maisie.'

He watched as Charles' eyes widened, his mouth dropping open. Then recognition dawned.

'Oh, my God. Nathan? I was not expecting to see you here!' He grasped Nathan's hand in a firm handshake. 'Look at you, all grown up now. I remember a time when you were shorter than me.' Then he turned to Bethany. 'And I recognise you, Bethany. You've barely changed.'

'Mr Skinner.' Bethany nodded at him. 'We wanted to talk to you. It's about Noah and Maisie.'

Charles' smile faded, and a look of sadness passed across his face. He sighed. 'I don't know why you would want to talk about them now. It's been years since they passed away.'

Nathan thought he had misheard. He glanced at Bethany, who looked equally confused.

'What did you say? Did you just say that Maisie and Noah are dead?'

'Yes. Didn't you know? My sister sent me a letter saying they died seven years ago. There was a bout of influenza at their house, and both my children…they succumbed to it.' Charles swallowed hard, looking close to tears. 'There's not a day goes by that I don't think about them. They were so young, and now they're gone.'

Nathan remembered Maisie talking about how they had no contact with their father after they went to their aunt's house. They wrote letters to him, but they never got an answer.

'Didn't you go and see them before they died?' Bethany demanded. 'Did you write to them?'

'I…I couldn't.' Charles looked very sheepish. 'They both wrote to me and said they didn't want to see me anymore. That they were living a better life and didn't want me around. I heard nothing after that until Lily told me they died.'

That would make sense from what Maisie and Noah had said. Lily had been pulling the strings in everything. Nathan could see that the man before them was broken, that he missed his children dearly. Even after everything, he wanted his children, and they were gone in his mind.

'Well, your sister has been lying to you,' he said.

'What?' Charles frowned. 'What do you mean?'

'Seven years ago, Maisie and Noah ran away. We found them and took them in. They've been living with us ever since.'

Nathan watched as Charles' face paled and, for a moment, thought he was going to keel over. Charles staggered over to the steps and sat down heavily.

'I... Are you telling me that...my children...they've been in Derby all this time?'

'We live in Chester Green,' Bethany said quietly. 'Just a couple of miles away.'

'I...I don't believe this.' Charles swallowed hard and rubbed at his chest. 'But Lily told me they died. Said that she had dealt with the bodies.'

'She must have done that to cover her tracks when they ran away in case you came up to the house,' Nathan remarked grimly. 'You would have discovered the truth, anyway.'

'Truth?'

'You didn't know how they were being treated?'

Charles shook his head. Nathan could tell he was really in the dark about what was going on. But he had to have known something if he sent his children away with his sister.

'Where are they now?' Charles croaked. 'My little ones. Where are they?'

'With us. And they've got questions.' Nathan folded his arms. 'You need to give them answers. They've been suffering all this time because you've not bothered to protect your children. I think they deserve to know why you treated them this way after their mother died. Because whatever you're going through is nothing compared to what they've experienced.'

Charles' shoulders slumped. He looked at the floor as he nodded. 'I understand,' he said quietly. 'After all, it's my fault they ended up in this position in the first place. I should have stopped this years ago.'

'Stopped what?' Bethany asked.

Charles glanced up at them, his expression haunted. 'Stopped my wife from dying years ago. This all started because of her death. And I allowed it to happen because I was scared.'

Bethany and Nathan glanced at each other. Nathan wanted to ask who Charles feared, but he had a feeling he knew the answer.

He feared his sister.

CHAPTER 9

Maisie's head was throbbing. She wanted to sleep, but it was not comfortable. Every time she closed her eyes and tried to lie down, she felt like she was going to be sick and had to sit up again. The doctor had told her this was normal, and she needed to rest, but Maisie felt too sluggish to rest. It wasn't helping at all.

But she couldn't do anything else. She couldn't read with the thought of it hurting her eyes, she couldn't have much light in her room without a headache, and the thought of having food made her nauseous. She couldn't get comfortable at all.

Noah had urged her to lie down and not worry about anything, something Maisie had scoffed at. Charlotte was still around. The woman had left the house and wasn't anywhere to be found, but she could easily come back.

Noah and Cook were looking around for her in case Charlotte was hiding in the house, and a police constable had been sent for. She should feel protected, but Maisie didn't. She just felt nauseous, worried that if she closed her eyes, something would happen again.

Even with the thought of being sick fresh in her mind, Maisie could feel sleep dragging her under. Noah had left a chamber pot by the bed in case she wanted to vomit, and Maisie was tempted to reach for it. She was going to be no use to anyone if she tried to do anything but sleep.

Shifting carefully onto her side, Maisie rested her head on the pillows and stared at the window. It was open to let a breeze in, showing a bright blue sky outside and the tops of trees. She could hear birds tweeting in the distance. That was surprisingly soothing, and Maisie found herself drifting off while she listened to it. It helped to close her eyes, and she felt sleep pulling her under.

Maybe she needed to exhaust herself enough just to pass out. The thought of sleep now didn't feel as uncomfortable.

Maisie awoke suddenly when she felt someone grab her arm. It was a fierce grip, fingers digging into her arm as she was hauled off the bed. Someone clamped a hand over her mouth and then tried to stuff something between her lips.

Maisie began to panic. She had no idea what was going on, but she wasn't about to go lying down. Pulling her head away from the cloth, she started to scream. A moment later, pain exploded in her face when someone slapped her.

'Shut up, you little brat!'

On the edge of her awareness, Maisie was sure that it was Charlotte. She had come back. And from the other person grabbing her, she wasn't alone.

A hand clamped over her mouth again, but Maisie struggled and flailed. She felt as if she was going to pass out, but she didn't stop. If she did, Charlotte was going to drag her out of there.

Where was Noah? And Nathan? Were they not back?

The edge of the hand missed her mouth, and Maisie bit down on the finger as hard as she could. There was a howl of pain, and the other attacker tried to pull his hand away, but Maisie held on. Charlotte attempted to grab at her, only for Maisie to get her legs out from under her and kick her in the stomach.

Charlotte stumbled back, falling to the ground as Maisie thrust an elbow into the man's chest. He let go of her, and Maisie practically fell off the bed. The world tilted around her. She scrambled to her feet and stumbled towards the door. She had to get out of there.

Whatever Charlotte had planned for her was not something she wanted to go through. She fell against the wall as she left the room. Her legs were shaking, and Maisie was struggling to keep upright. But she tried screaming again. 'Help! Help me!'

'Maisie!'

The sound of running feet reached her ears, and then Nathan was there, hurrying down the hall towards her. He grabbed Maisie before she ended up on the floor, hauling her into his arms.

'What's going on?'

'In...in there...' Maisie pointed towards her room. 'Charlotte...she...she...'

She didn't get any further before she passed out, Nathan's voice fading as she sunk into the blackness.

*   *   *

'You're telling us that our father is alive, and he's here?' Noah demanded.

Nathan nodded. 'He thought the two of you were dead. That's what Lily said to him.'

'And he would trust his sister's word,' Noah grunted, pacing around the table. 'But he never came to question it all? Why wouldn't he try to find us, anyway?'

Nathan looked at Maisie, who was sitting at the kitchen table with her hands wrapped around a steaming mug. She looked less pale than she had been a short while ago, but the sight of her was concerning. The tumble down the stairs and then the attack had taken a lot out of her.

'I think that's what you need to discuss with your father,' he said grimly. 'He needs to tell you what really happened.'

'What do you mean?' Maisie asked, lifting her head to stare at him.

'There's more to this than you realise. And it's...' Nathan grimaced. 'Worse than you think.'

Charles had told Nathan and Bethany everything on the way back to the house. To say he was shocked by what had truly happened was an understatement. Nathan couldn't believe someone could be so cold about what was going on. To think that all of them had been victims of one person and they couldn't get away.

Hopefully, this would make things right. Maisie and Noah were not children anymore. They could cope with it.

'What is worse than we think?' Noah snapped back. 'Why don't you tell us?'

Nathan took a deep breath. 'It's best to hear it from your father. He can answer further questions.' He looked at Maisie. 'Do you think you can talk to him with how you're feeling? We can wait...'

'I don't want to wait.' There was a finality to her response, her gaze unblinking as she looked up at him. 'I want to know what's been going on and why he did this to us. We've suffered enough, and I think we deserve an explanation.'

From her tone and her expression, Nathan knew there was no chance of asking her to back down. She was going to do this regardless of whoever was there. And he couldn't blame her; after all, Maisie deserved to know why her aunt wanted to get her back to Buxton after years away.

Noah looked unhappy about it, but he nodded and went over to his sister. 'Let's do this together,' he said, resting a hand on her shoulder. 'We'll speak to him in here. I don't want you moving more than you must.'

Maisie gave him a small smile. Nathan wished he knew what

to say. It hurt him to see her in such a state when she was normally so strong. He went into the living room and found Charles standing by the window, staring out into the street. Bethany was on the settee, sitting awkwardly as she watched him. Squeezing his sister's shoulder as he went past, Nathan joined Charles at the window.

'I walk by here every day,' Charles said, never taking his eyes off the street. 'To go to work, I pass by this area. To think my children were so close…'

'They will talk to you,' Nathan said gruffly. 'But Maisie is not able to be moved too much. She was attacked earlier.'

Charles spun around, his face paling. 'What? She was attacked? Who by?'

'Your aunt's maid. She got a job here this morning, and then she attacked Maisie twice. She's currently at the police station being questioned about it.'

Nathan couldn't describe the rage he felt at coming to Maisie's room and seeing the two would-be intruders attempting to leave. One of them had got away, but Nathan snagged Charlotte before she could escape, pinning her on the floor until Noah arrived to deal with her. Nathan was surprised his friend didn't beat the woman, especially with the way she had been verbally goading him, but Noah had a lot more restraint than Nathan thought possible.

'Oh, God.' Charles swallowed. 'It wasn't anything to do with their running away from Lily's, was it?'

'The police will find out about that. Right now, you need to explain everything to your children. They deserve to know the truth.' Nathan glanced at Bethany. 'It's not my place to tell them, not unless you're unable to.'

'I don't want to, but I think it's better coming from me.' Charles absently adjusted his jacket, squaring his shoulders. 'Take me to them. I think it's about time I saw my children again.'

Hoping that he would not regret this, Nathan led the older

man back to the kitchen. Maisie and Noah were sitting at the kitchen table, Cook pouring more tea for them. They all looked up as the men entered, and Nathan felt the definitive chill in the air. Noah's expression was stony as he straightened up.

'So, you are alive,' he said stiffly.

Charles cleared his throat, and Nathan glanced over, only to be surprised when he saw the tears in the man's eyes.

'I…' Charles managed a tiny smile. 'I suppose I deserved that.'

'Yes. You did.' Noah rubbed Maisie's back, his eyes never leaving his father. Maisie was also staring at Charles. 'You left us with that monster because of your debts. You practically sold us to Aunt Lily, all because you couldn't manage your money.'

Charles' shoulders slumped, and he was silent as he drew out a chair across from his children. He sat down slowly, and Nathan could see the tiredness. Something had been pressing down on his shoulders for a long time.

'I didn't send you to Lily because of my debts. I didn't have any debts.'

Nathan watched as Noah and Maisie's expressions turned to confusion. Maisie was the one who spoke first. 'That…that doesn't make sense. We constantly heard you shouting at Mother when she complained about your gambling habits…'

'There was someone in the family with a gambling habit, yes, but it wasn't me.' Charles took a deep breath. 'It was Lily.'

Maisie's eyes widened. 'What? Aunt Lily is the gambler?'

'She was always doing it. Didn't matter what she was gambling on, it was the thrill of doing it. She started spending more than they had, and if her husband knew about it…well, you know how harsh he can be.' Charles stared at his hands on the table. 'I was covering the money she gambled so he wouldn't find out. That's why we were having financial problems of our own.'

'You were covering for her all the time,' Noah said grimly.

'She's family, Noah. If Maisie was in a similar situation, wouldn't you help her as much as you could?'

'I would've made sure she didn't put herself in that position in the first place.'

Charles winced, and Nathan saw him tense before he slumped again.

'I suppose I deserved that.'

'Did Mother know about it?'

'Of course she did. What did you think we were fighting about? I would help my little sister. And Eloise…she hated that I was getting her out of trouble and forgetting that we had a family. That the money should go to something more worthwhile, like looking after you two. I wanted to stop, but Lily…' Charles grimaced. 'She's a vindictive soul. All she cares about is money. And being in control. Having those two things just made her dangerous. As I found out, to my detriment.'

Nathan could feel the hairs prickle on the back of his neck. He knew what was coming next, and it was still shocking to him. Maisie and Noah glanced at each other.

'What do you mean by that?' Maisie asked. 'Are you…?'

'The day your mother died, Lily was at the house. She wanted more money, but I had already told her that I wouldn't help her anymore. She came to the house to confront me, to tell me I was a terrible brother who didn't care about his family. Eloise got involved and told her off with some very strong words. She reminded Lily that we had a family, and she should have stopped her gambling problem years ago. She even said she would tell Lily's husband what had happened.' Charles rubbed his hands over his face. 'Lily was furious at that. She doesn't like being told what to do.'

Noah was pale. Maisie looked as if she was going to pass out again. Nathan moved around to her side of the table and placed his hands on her shoulders, nodding at Cook. 'Could you make Maisie some tea with plenty of sugar, please? She's just had a massive shock.'

'Yes, sir.'

As Cook moved away from the table, Nathan felt Maisie tremble under his hands. Was she crying? Her voice sounded clear, though, as she addressed her father.

'Are you trying to tell us that it was Aunt Lily who pushed our mother down the stairs?' she asked. 'She wasn't at the house that day.'

'She was. She and Eloise got into a fight, with Lily following Eloise when she went to check on you and Noah. They argued at the top of the stairs, and Lily...she just pushed...' Charles broke off, his face screwing up as he fought with himself. 'Then your mother...she was...'

'She was dead,' Noah said in a low growl. Nathan could feel the anger simmering off him. 'And you covered up for her instead of telling the authorities what happened.'

'I didn't want Lily to be arrested for an accident.'

'You were covering for her, yet again. You put her above your family.'

'That's exactly what Nathan said to me.' Charles glanced up at Nathan with a haunted look. 'He did have a ring of truth to his words. He might have hit me, and his words would have had more effect on me.'

'I wish I could hit you right now,' Noah snapped. 'You put us through all of that and housed us with a murderer. What possessed you to do that?'

Charles blinked several times before fumbling in his pocket for a handkerchief. He pressed it to his face for a moment, Nathan sensing he was taking a bit of time to compose himself. Given what he had heard already, he could understand why. Maisie and Noah hadn't liked any of this news, but this was going to be worse.

'Lily threatened me.'

'What could Aunt Lily have threatened you with?' Maisie demanded.

'During our loud argument, I said that I wouldn't help her

anymore. I was putting my foot down. I was going to keep my resolve even after Eloise died, but then Lily...' Charles lowered his hands, staring at the yellowing handkerchief in his palms. 'She said if I didn't give her money, she was going to the authorities and say that I committed murder by pushing my wife down the stairs. She can tell a convincing story. I've seen it many times over the years, since we were children. She would make it look like I did it in cold blood. If I didn't want that, I was to keep sending her money.' He hesitated. 'And you two were collateral. You were to stay with her to make sure I did as I was told. If I was late on a payment, she would go to the police or have something happen to you.'

Noah's mouth dropped open. 'She really didn't care that she was threatening the lives of children?'

'Money was all that Lily ever cared about. I don't think she ever loved her husband. It was all about the money, and she let greed take over.' Charles shook his head. 'A month ago, I had had enough. I had lost my wife, and I believed I lost my children, and I was still sending Lily money. I told her no more, and she threatened me with the usual, but this time, I said to go right ahead. At this point, I don't care anymore. If she wants me arrested for Eloise's death, then she can do it. I haven't got anything to live for. I believed you two were dead years ago because she told me.'

'You trusted her too much,' Noah said gruffly.

His father nodded. Nathan could feel the pain in the air. All three of them were feeling anguish over the fourteen years they missed because of one woman's greed for more money.

'I...I need some air.' Maisie shakily got to her feet. 'I...I can't...'

'Maisie...'

But Maisie headed to the door and stepped outside, barely looking back as her brother called after her. Charles shook his head.

'Leave her be for now, Noah. She needs a moment. What I've told you is a lot.'

Nathan could argue with that, but he was more worried about Maisie. He pressed a hand on his friend's shoulder. 'Talk to your father. And don't try anything stupid. Much as you want to admit it, he's not your enemy.'

'Speak for yourself,' Noah muttered.

Nathan didn't answer that, leaving the kitchen after Maisie.

CHAPTER 10

Maisie's heart felt like it was bursting out of her chest. She could barely breathe, and her body wouldn't stop shaking. It was like she wasn't in control of herself anymore.

Her mother had been killed by Lily. It wasn't an accident. Lily was the gambler, and she was the one who took Maisie and Noah away. And her father had let it all happen because he cared too much about his sister. He had put her over his family more times than he should have, and his family had paid the price.

She had always thought her father didn't care about her because there was no contact at all. That he got rid of them because he didn't want them around. Lily had made sure they were isolated.

Her aunt was a monster.

'Maisie.'

Maisie turned when she heard Nathan's voice, but she wobbled and almost fell. Nathan caught her before she hit the ground, cradling her against his chest. It felt warm and comforting, and Maisie allowed that moment to lean against him, her forehead against his chest. She didn't know whether to scream or cry, maybe both. Nathan held her, rubbing her back as he did. Maisie managed to get her footing back, wrapping her arms around his waist as she resisted the urge to cry.

They stayed like that for a while. Maisie was aware they could be seen if someone came along, but she didn't care. She just wanted to be in Nathan's arms, even if it was for a few minutes. She needed this.

'I'm sorry,' Nathan said quietly.

'What are you sorry about?'

'That you had to go through that. You were a victim of your aunt's greed. And she took advantage of your father's love for her.'

'She did more than that.' Maisie lifted her head. 'She tore everyone's lives apart. She killed my mother, took my brother and me away and made us work like slaves, and then she was going to separate us because we wanted to run away.'

'She doesn't care about anyone except herself. The money is all she ever wanted.' Nathan frowned. 'Was she always like this? Did she always prefer money over familial relationships?'

'I don't know. We didn't have much interaction with her when we were children. Despite Father spending a lot of time with her, we barely saw her except at Christmas. And I believe we were at her wedding reception, but that was it.' Maisie peered up at him. 'Do you think there was a reason for that? Did my parents keep us away from Aunt Lily?'

'It's a possibility that your father was aware of how bad your aunt was and kept you out of the way. Or it could have been your mother refusing to allow you to be anywhere near a bad influence.'

'With the way things went in our childhood, I'm willing to believe it was the latter.' Maisie wanted to stay in Nathan's arms for longer but she was struggling to concentrate, so she reluctantly released him. 'I knew she didn't like Father's family, and she wanted to prevent us from being corrupted as well.'

'Is that what you believe?'

'I heard Father arguing about it when I was about…six years old? It stuck with me at the time.' Maisie went to a nearby bench and sat down heavily. 'The last time I saw my grandparents was about then. I thought they were nice but rather pushy. I was uncomfortable with it, I seem to remember. Noah was more vocal about it. Then Mother put her foot down and said we wouldn't be going anywhere near his parents, especially if Father kept putting us in dangerous situations.'

'Dangerous?' Nathan looked surprised at that. 'What did they do?'

'I don't really know. I just remember having a day out with them and meeting various new people who made me uncomfortable. I think we must have been accosted by people Grandpa owed money to.'

'He was a gambler, too?'

'Aunt Lily often played cards whenever she had guests over for dinner. Then she would talk about how her father taught her how to play.' Maisie shrugged. 'It's a stab in the dark, but I'm guessing Grandpa spent more than he had as well.'

'The only person who can answer that is your father.'

Maisie snorted. 'That man is weak. He couldn't stand up for his family against his parents or his sister. If he had done that, we wouldn't have gotten separated. Maybe Mother…' Her voice caught, and she forced herself to carry on. 'Maybe she would still be alive.'

Nathan didn't say anything for a moment. Then he approached the bench and sat beside her. His thigh was warm up against hers, and Maisie immediately leaned into him, resting her head on his shoulder.

Nathan slipped an arm around her shoulders, and they sat in silence for a while. The only sound came from the breeze in the trees. It was a beautifully warm day, but Maisie felt cold. The breeze was making her shiver.

'Do you want to go back inside?' Nathan asked.

'No. Not just yet.' Maisie squeezed her eyes shut to stop herself from crying, but that just hurt them. 'Lily used Mother's death to her advantage. She practically kidnapped us and used us to get more money out of Father.'

'It would seem to. Even though he might not have shown it, that man loved you and Noah.'

'He certainly had a strange way of showing it.' Maisie sat up and rubbed her eyes. 'Why say we were dead, though? And why would Charlotte turn up here years later?'

Nathan shifted on the bench and sat back.

'I think it was to make sure Charles didn't turn up at the house. He would have demanded to see you, and Lily didn't want him to see your state and how she hadn't been looking after you.'

'And that was after he received letters, supposedly from us, saying we never wanted to see him again,' Maisie murmured.

'Just so.'

'But why would Charlotte appear here now? Why would she think to look here for us? I don't understand that part.'

Nathan shook his head. 'The only way to get that answer is to talk to Lily herself unless Charlotte confesses to why she came here in the first place. But there is no chance I'm letting Lily anywhere near you.'

'Why not?' Maisie demanded. 'She did all of this to us, and we suffered for more than a decade with her behaviour and antics. I think we deserve more than an explanation as to why she would put Noah and me through all of that. We were children, not bargaining tools. We shouldn't have been put in that position.'

'I understand that…'

'Do you? Really?'

Nathan sat up. 'Of course I do. Do you think I'm sitting here doing nothing? I'm trying to figure out how they found out where you were in the first place. Did they find out by coincidence, or…'

He left it hanging in the air, but Maisie knew what he was talking about. Her heart sank.

'Or did she know where we were the whole time? That she was still using us as collateral, but from a different place?'

'There is that possibility.'

Now Maisie was feeling cold. She wrapped her arms around herself and began to shiver, unable to get rid of the chill. Nathan stood up and began to take off his jacket.

'What are you doing?'

'I'm being a gentleman.' He draped the jacket around her shoulders. 'And I don't care if anyone sees us right now. I'm more worried about you.'

'I'm fine.'

'You're shaking to the point you're behaving as if you're in the middle of winter.' Nathan rested his hands on her shoulders. 'I know this is a lot for you to take in. You've had a rough day. You were attacked, for a start. This was too much to put on your shoulders all at once, and that's my fault. I'm sorry about that.'

Maisie couldn't blame him for any of that. Neither of them knew it was going to happen. But the thought of Aunt Lily knowing exactly where she was without even bothering to look and was waiting in the wings, ready to make her move, left her scared. They had managed to run away from her, but she had known where they were all this time? Aunt Lily was showing herself to be more dangerous than anyone gave her credit for.

'I want to confront her.'

'What?' Nathan looked startled. 'Confront her?'

'I think she needs that. To see what she's done.' Maisie drew in a deep breath. 'That woman has messed our lives up, and she doesn't care. I want to confront her about it.'

Nathan shook his head. 'I don't know if that is such a good idea.'

'Why not?' Maisie huffed.

'I doubt she's going to listen to you on any of that. She doesn't care about anyone else's opinion, does she? She might have found someone just as mean to be her husband, but I doubt they care about each other or how they feel.'

'She cared enough to not want her husband to know about her gambling,' Maisie pointed out.

'Unless it wasn't her money to begin with. Business and personal accounts are often separate.'

'You think she started dipping into the business accounts and didn't want her husband to find out about it?'

Nathan shrugged. 'It's a possibility. I don't know how her husband doesn't know about it, given how much money she's been asking for, but she must have gotten herself into such a deep hole that she can't stop. And the money she sneaks from her husband goes towards her debts while the money from her brother gets put back into the accounts.'

Maisie pressed her fingers to her temples.

'God, this is making my head hurt even more. This is too much for me to take in.'

'I'm sorry, Maisie.'

'It's not your fault. None of this was.'

Nathan shifted from foot to foot, shoving his hands in his pockets. 'I brought your father in. I wanted to confront him about what was going on. In my head, I thought things were going to come together, and we'd find a solution, but it just feels like a worse mess than before.' He stared at the ground as he hung his head. 'I guess I'm not that good as a solicitor if I'm opening up more problems than there were.'

Maisie couldn't be upset at him for any of what he did. She was annoyed that she hadn't been given any warning that her father was turning up, but that was not Nathan's fault. He was too kind-hearted to do anything so harsh. She cupped his jaw in her hand. Nathan looked up, surprise flickering behind his eyes.

'I was never going to blame you for that,' she said gently. 'I would if it was my aunt, but not my father. However, it's a lot for me to take in right now.'

'That's understood.' Nathan swallowed. Did he just lean into her hand a little, or was that his imagination? 'What are you going to do now?'

'I don't know yet.'

But Maisie did know. She just wasn't about to tell him that just yet.

* * *

It felt like forever before everyone was asleep and the house was silent. Maisie lay in bed, trying to keep herself calm as she thought about what she was going to do. It was going to be mad and dangerous to do it on her own, but it had to be done. None of her family was going to be safe unless she did something about it.

Nathan had mentioned getting a solicitor, someone from his firm, to represent the family to confront Aunt Lily and make her back off, but Maisie didn't think that would work. Not with the threat she had made regarding Charles and his wife's death. She could easily turn it around. Even though it was fourteen years later, there was a chance Charles could be hanged for the death, and Maisie wasn't about to go through all of that.

She had to do this herself.

Dressing as silently as she could, she tiptoed out of her room and made her way down to the side door. She breathed a sigh of relief once she stepped out. She never liked moving around as if she was committing a crime. Besides, everything always felt incredibly loud at that time of night.

The moon was out and high in the sky as Maisie moved into the street, wrapping her coat around her. It was still warm, but not as warm as during the day. There was a definite chill in the air, and it made Maisie shiver.

She tried to ignore it as she made her way down the street, hurrying from streetlamp to streetlamp. There was nobody around, and she didn't want to get cornered by anyone. At the end of the street, regular cabs passed by, so it wouldn't take much for her to stick a hand out to wave one down. If they were paid handsomely enough, they would take her to Buxton.

Hopefully, because Maisie just about had enough money on her to take her one way. When she was in Buxton, she was going to struggle, but she would think about that once she got there.

'Maisie!'

Maisie spun around with a gasp. Noah was trotting towards her, moving out of the shadows as he tried to get his breath back.

'Noah! What are you doing out here?'

'I was going to ask you the same question.' Noah stared back at her. 'What do you think you're doing? Why are you sneaking away at this time of night?'

Maisie thought about lying to him, but Noah would figure it out quickly. He knew her better than anyone else. She looked around. 'I was going to see Aunt Lily.'

'What?' Noah looked incredulous. 'Why on earth would you do that? Are you mad?'

'I want to get some answers from her. To know why she did all of this.'

'We know why she did this! She's a greedy, manipulative woman who cares more about where the money is coming from than her own family. She murdered her sister-in-law and was willing to keep us as hostages to make her brother pay more money!' Noah waved his hands around in the air. 'You should be staying as far away from that woman as possible. She's the reason we spent our childhood being treated as badly as we did.'

'I still want to talk to her and know why she did it,' Maisie argued. 'I want to hear it from her.'

'How is that going to make anything better?'

'I don't know, but I want to try.' Maisie hesitated. 'Stupid as it may sound, I want to hear her be remorseful. That she regrets any of this. If she does regret it, then there may be hope to actually help her.'

'Help?' Noah stared at her with his mouth open. 'You want to help the woman who put us through all of that? The woman who beat us and starved us?'

'I know it sounds foolish…'

'Of course it's foolish! You shouldn't be anywhere near her! She'll take you back to Buxton, lock you up, and never let you out again!'

'Don't be dramatic…'

'I don't want to lose my sister, Maisie!' Noah was practically shouting now. 'I lost Mother, and I practically lost Father. I'm not about to lose you, too.'

Maisie felt the tears prickling in her eyes. She hated seeing her brother like this. She took his hands as he waved them around and held them until he stopped shaking. His breathing was ragged, but it was better than before.

'I need to do this for myself, Noah. It's not something I can push to one side. I need to look her in the eye and ask her why.'

'How would that make things any better?'

'I'll find out when I get there.'

Noah's jaw tightened, and he looked at a point over her shoulder. Then he sighed. 'All right. But you won't need to go to Buxton. I happen to know that Aunt Lily is in Derby.'

'What? How?'

'I overheard the police constables when they were putting Charlotte into the back of their carriage. They mentioned Kedleston Hall and how it was only a stone's throw away from Derby. It's right on the edge of the city.'

Just on the edge of the city. That meant Maisie wouldn't have to worry about getting stuck in Buxton again. She looked around, seeing a couple of carriages nearby. They had to be fine with taking her that far.

'Fancy a trip to Kedleston Hall to talk to Aunt Lily?' she asked. 'I think it's best if we have that conversation together.'

'Right now?'

'Yes. She will be on the back foot if we talk to her in the middle of the night. After all, she's given us plenty of discomfort, hasn't she? Might as well make the most of it and give her a taste of her own medicine.'

Noah arched an eyebrow, looking bemused. 'I don't know whether to find that impressive or worrying coming from you, Maisie.'

'Think of it as both.'

'What are you two doing?'

Maisie's heart sank when she heard Nathan's voice. He appeared behind Noah, shrugging into his jacket with his hair still standing on end. He looked from his friend to Maisie and back again.

'Would you two like to explain why you're in the middle of the street at this time of night? Or am I going to have to guess?'

CHAPTER 11

When Nathan half-stirred during the night to get a fresh glass of water, he heard someone moving around. With his nerves on edge because of the attack earlier in the day, Nathan had grabbed a knife from the kitchen table to find the intruder, only to see Noah slip out of the side door.

For a moment, he thought his friend was going to see Beatrice, but that seemed ridiculous. It was the middle of the night, and Beatrice would be asleep. Noah wasn't stupid enough to get the woman he loved into some sort of trouble.

He just had to be sure that he was behaving himself. Although it seemed strange to have a late-night stroll.

Leaving the knife in the kitchen, Nathan hurried back to his room. He had fallen asleep at his desk after going through some files, so he was still dressed. He just needed to get his jacket and then he could chase after Noah. Hopefully, he wasn't out of sight by the time Nathan got down to the street.

Sure enough, when he stepped outside and looked down the street, he saw Noah at the corner. He seemed to be in a heated conversation with someone. The gas lamp shone a light over the woman's face, and Nathan realised it was Maisie. What was she doing out here? Had Noah seen her and followed her out?

Nathan wondered if both were up to something. They had been very quiet in the last few hours before retiring. Noah had carried on his duties as normal, while Maisie remained in her room. Nathan had checked on both before going to his room, and they were rather quiet. Had Maisie been planning this when he was talking to her?

He approached them.

'What are you two doing?'

Maisie saw him first, and her face lost its colour. Noah turned, his expression sheepish. Nathan looked from him to Maisie and back again.

'Would you two like to explain why you're in the middle of the street at this time of night? Or am I going to have to guess?'

'We want to confront Aunt Lily about her behaviour,' Maisie said before Noah could open his mouth. 'She's done a lot of things to us, and we deserve a proper explanation.'

'But you know what the explanation is,' Nathan reminded her. 'She's the greedy gambler who demands money from her brother, and he's too weak to say no, so she used you and Noah to make sure he keeps paying.'

'I want to hear it from her.' Maisie sounded defiant on that. 'She put us through it all. We were children. I think we deserve to hear why she would do it.'

'And what good will that do?'

Maisie didn't answer. Noah looked stony-faced. Nathan could tell neither of them was going to back down on this. They were going whether he let them or not.

'You're going all the way to Buxton to confront her?'

'She's at Kedleston Hall, Nathan,' Noah answered. 'Not that far at all. It seems like the ideal opportunity to talk to her.'

God, the pair of them were stubborn. Nathan could see he

wasn't going to win on this. Sighing, he beckoned them to follow him. 'Come on back to the house. We can use the carriage.'

'What?' Maisie frowned. 'Why would we use your carriage?'

'Because I'm coming with you, that's why.'

His friends exchanged surprised glances, and then Maisie was shaking her head. 'No, you should stay here.'

'Why should I? This has affected my family as well, hasn't it?'

'Well...'

'There are no arguments about this, Maisie,' Nathan cut her off. 'If you two go alone, there's a chance you could get caught up in trouble. I'm going with you to make sure that doesn't happen.'

'But...' Maisie began, and Nathan held up a hand.

'Stop. I told you I'm going with you. If you don't like it, that's fine, but you'll stay here. You're not sneaking off in the middle of the night to see her.'

Maisie squared her shoulders as she drew herself up. 'You would have stopped us if we went in the daytime,' she said. 'We do have chores as well.'

'You don't have to worry about that. We just need to speak to Bethany, and you'll have the day off to deal with it, even if she's not happy about it.' Nathan shook his head, running his fingers through his hair. 'This is not ideal for either of you. You go at this time of night, you're not going to get to see her, and you'll be thrown off the property. It's best to go during the day and with someone likely to get you inside.'

Noah snorted. 'You would be able to get us into the house?'

'The Earl of Kedleston is one of my colleague's clients. He knows me, so I'm sure he would allow me into the house.' Nathan shrugged. 'I'm sure he would want to know he has a cruel, vindictive woman as a guest, anyway.'

Maisie huffed and folded her arms. 'That's one way to say we wouldn't be able to get what we want if we went alone. Nobody's going to listen to a couple of servants.'

'Oh, he'll listen. It's just getting into the house itself that will be a problem. If you're not thrown off the estate entirely.' Nathan sighed. 'Look, Maisie, just come back in and rest. We'll go to Kedleston Hall in the morning when we're more awake and thinking more clearly. You can have a better plan on what to say to her instead of being impulsive.'

'He's right, Maisie,' Noah said before Maisie could protest. 'We need to think about this more carefully. We know how wily Aunt Lily is. It's something we have to have a plan for.'

Maisie sniffed. 'I was going to have a plan,' she argued. 'I would sort it out in the carriage on the way over.'

Nathan shook his head. That was not going to work, not in his experience. He glanced at Noah and gave him a silent nod. Sensing that he was to make himself scarce, Noah started walking back to the house. Nathan stepped towards Maisie and took her hands, glad that she didn't pull away from him.

'Maisie, you're going to hurt yourself further if you carry on like this,' he said gently.

'Why would you say that?'

'You were attacked and hurt twice today…'

'You make it sound like I've forgotten about that,' Maisie replied hotly. 'I am perfectly aware of who attacked me as well.'

'Then you know that you need to rest. You're acting impulsively instead of rationally.'

Maisie scoffed at him. 'You get pushed down the stairs and have someone attempt to kidnap you, then you decide if this is rational or not,' she shot back.

'Maisie…'

'She stole years of my life with her greed and cruelty, Nathan. Half of my childhood. We suffered because of her and that man she married. Do you think I can sit back and let her carry on?'

'That's not what I'm saying.'

'Then what are you saying?'

Nathan didn't care that anyone could see them. He wrapped his arms around her and drew Maisie close. She tensed, but she didn't push him away. She was just stiff in his embrace for a while, with Nathan simply holding her. He rested his chin on her head and slowly rubbed her back. After a while, he felt the tension fading away, and she eventually sagged against him. Finally, her arms went around him, and he felt her grip tightening.

Then he heard her starting to cry. That made his heartbreak, and he kissed her head.

'It's all right. I'm here,' he whispered. 'I'm always going to be here.'

As far as he was concerned, he wasn't going to let her go.

* * *

MAISIE DIDN'T WANT to admit it, but a night of sleep and something to eat in the morning did make her feel better. Despite the headache, she had a clearer mind. It wasn't ideal to be running around as she had been the day before; she was too emotional. Resting and taking care of herself helped with what she needed to do.

She was still going to confront her aunt, and Nathan said he wouldn't stop her. But she needed to be more logical about it. And going alone in the middle of the night was definitely not that. It was best to do it when things were clearer for everyone.

Maisie hoped he was right about that. She needed to do this, to face that woman one more time. If they didn't tell her to go away, there was a chance that she would send someone else to come after Maisie or Noah. Aunt Lily was determined to get them back, and all for the money. She couldn't let her aunt do that.

After breakfast, Nathan, Noah, and Maisie headed over to

Kedleston Hall. It was a huge building at the top of a hill with sloping green fields all around it. There was a river that ran through a part of the estate, covered by a bridge they rode over.

Maisie looked at the hill beside the house and wondered what the view would be like from up there. Given the surrounding area, the family could probably see for miles around.

How on earth had Aunt Lily become friends with the family who lived here? Nathan had said they were decent folk who had always been respectful towards them in the past, but nothing to suggest they would associate with a regular, working-class woman like Aunt Lily. But then he noted he was a heavy gambler as well, and he was a shareholder in the business their uncle ran, and it all made sense after that.

Maisie hoped they wouldn't have to be confronted by the Kedleston family, either; otherwise, this was going to get uncomfortable for more than just them.

As their carriage pulled into the courtyard, three horses trotted into view. One was ridden by a gentleman dressed in dove-grey, and one was ridden by a lady in a matching dress. The third rider was Aunt Lily. Maisie hadn't even realised her aunt could ride a horse. Her expression froze when she saw Maisie and Noah get out of the carriage, her face so pale Maisie thought she was going to fall out of the saddle.

'Mr North!' Lord Kedleston approached them, still on horseback. 'Good morning!'

'Good morning, my lord.' Nathan shielded his eyes from the sun. 'Out for a ride, were you?'

'With an estate like ours, we like to make the most of it. Very bracing as well. Anyway, what are you doing here? I wasn't aware of an appointment with my solicitor this morning.'

'Actually, we came to see your guest.' Nathan indicated Aunt Lily. 'It's about some family matters that need her immediate attention.'

Lord Kedleston frowned. 'Oh, really?'

'Do you mind if we have a few words with her right now? It can't wait, I'm afraid.'

'I think you'll have to ask my guest.' The earl turned in his saddle. 'Lily, did you have business with my law firm? I wasn't aware of it.'

'I...it was a last-minute thing, my lord,' Aunt Lily said hurriedly. She trotted over and dismounted. 'I'll speak to them here. I won't be long.'

'Are you sure?'

'It's just a couple of minor bits of paperwork we were discussing,' Nathan said quickly. 'I promise we won't take up much of her time.'

Maisie was hoping that Aunt Lily would say something that meant she could retort with a remark that would bring her behaviour to the man's attention, but her aunt knew better and kept quiet. She didn't look at her host, busying herself with the reins as Lord Kedleston and the lady Maisie guessed was his wife trotted away. Then Aunt Lily swung around on the three of them, her eyes flashing.

'What is the meaning of this?' she hissed. 'Who are you?'

'I'm a friend of Maisie and Noah's,' Nathan replied, barely blinking. 'They wanted to talk to you.'

'What about? Unless it's an apology for running away, I've got nothing to say to them.'

'We want you to leave us alone,' Noah said.

Aunt Lily raised her eyebrows. 'Leave you alone? Why would I do that? You came to me to work off your father's death, and you're not anywhere near done.'

Noah snorted. 'We worked for you for nearly seven years. Given how little you were paying us, we must have paid it off and then some. You think we're going to go back where you're treating us atrociously and use us as some sort of collateral?'

'What are you talking about?'

'You took us so you could ensure Father would send money to

you, didn't you?' Maisie said, watching her aunt's face. 'You also told him if he stopped sending money, you would hurt us and make sure the police knew it was him who killed our mother by pushing her down the stairs. When we all know that it was you who did it.'

Aunt Lily's mouth fell open. She looked shocked. 'What…how dare you?' she gasped. 'How could you accuse me of that?'

'Father told us what you threatened to do,' Noah said sternly. 'All over it.'

'What?'

'Nathan found him for us.' Maisie placed a hand on Nathan's arm. It gave her some strength to continue when her heart was racing. 'He told us you said we were dead years when we ran away, but he still had the threat of being arrested for a crime he never committed hanging over his head. Last month, he said he was not sending you money anymore. He was fed up with it all, having lost his wife and children to you because of your selfishness. So, you decided to bring us back from the dead and look for us.'

'That's why you had Charlotte at the house, wasn't it?' Nathan continued. 'You found out where Maisie and Noah were, and you made sure Charlotte got a job at the house as well so she could get close and kidnap them.'

Aunt Lily looked as if she was about to lose her temper, but Maisie could see her panicking. They had hit close to the mark.

'I can't believe you would accuse me of that,' she cried. 'I would never do such a thing! Whatever Charlotte did was without my authority…'

'Charlotte talked in police custody,' Nathan cut her off.

Aunt Lily faltered. 'What?'

Maisie tried not to stare at Nathan. She knew he was attempting to bluff, but he hadn't said how. It was best to let him get on with it and hope that she didn't look like she was in the dark as well.

'Charlotte talked to the constables who took her away. She said you were the one who managed to find where your niece and nephew were and decided to find a way to use that to your advantage again, especially if your brother had finally cut you off after years of enabling your behaviour. You were going to kidnap them back, bring them in front of Charles Skinner, and threaten him once more.' Nathan shrugged. 'As long as you had your money coming in, you didn't care who you hurt, even if they were your flesh and blood. And you always could rely on your weak-willed older brother to look after you.'

Maisie watched as Aunt Lily's face went from bright red to white and back to red before turning green. She looked as if she was going to stand up to them and argue, but Nathan and Noah were a lot taller than her. They both towered over her, and Aunt Lily was not looking as big and scary as she had been before.

That made her feel more confident.

'We're not toys for you to mess around with, Aunt Lily,' Maisie said. 'We suffered because of your greed, and we're fed up with it. We just wanted to grow up with a loving family, and you tore that apart. All because you thought money was more important than your brother having a family. And you took that away from him.'

'But money is more important!' Aunt Lily cried.

'More important than your own husband?' Maisie shot back. 'Uncle Thomas wasn't the nicest of people, but I'm sure he wouldn't be impressed to hear that.'

'He would understand. He's just like me when it comes to that.' Her aunt looked away, her shoulders slumping. 'He gave me an allowance, but it's never enough. He kept a tight rein on things, and the money disappeared quickly. After a while, he had to make sure there was money for housekeeping that the housekeeper herself looked after. I still had an allowance, but I had to have it closely guarded so I didn't overspend.'

'So you went to your brother,' Noah said bitterly. 'Someone

who wasn't in a better financial position than your own husband and had a family to feed.'

'I'm his sister, and he promised that he would always look after me. When I told him I needed money, he gave it to me without question.'

'Despite the fact you were making us starve?'

Aunt Lily sniffed. 'If you were starving, maybe he shouldn't have had children. Anyway, your mother didn't like it. Especially once I owed more money than I could handle. I was getting desperate; it needed to be paid off, or my husband would find out. Charles was about to pay it, but then Eloise said absolutely not, and I was on my own. We argued, and I…'

She broke off, but Maisie knew where this was going.

'You pushed her down the stairs,' she murmured.

'It was an accident! I didn't mean to hurt her, but she…it just…' Aunt Lily glanced away. 'Charles said it was an accident, trying to protect me, and then he told me he wasn't going to give me any more money. Eloise had told him his family came first, and it was money that had caused her death. So, he was going to honour it. I panicked, and I threatened to tell the police he killed her if he didn't give me more money. Charles could easily fold for me. I knew how to wrap him around my finger. Adding his brats to the mix ensured he wouldn't stop anytime soon.'

'And you abused us in the process,' Noah snarled.

'I wanted to get rid of you, but I had followed through on keeping you as collateral, and now I was stuck with you.' Aunt Lily sounded bitter about it. 'Trust me, it wasn't a fun time for me, either.'

'I'm sure it wasn't,' Maisie sneered.

Her aunt didn't look like the bully they remembered from before. She looked like a little old lady who was losing her hold on the situation. Nathan gently nudged Maisie towards the carriage before facing Aunt Lily himself.

'Maisie and Noah want nothing to do with you,' he said. 'They managed to get away before the abuse you were handing to them killed them. And your brother...let's just say he's more than prepared to cut you off.'

'What?'

'You told him that his children were dead, and he's regretted his decisions ever since. Now he knows they're alive, he's not going to risk losing them again. You're done, as far as he's concerned.'

Aunt Lily's mouth fell open. She spluttered.

'What? What about my money?'

'You're going to have to figure that out for yourself. Your greed tore your brother's family apart, and he's not about to risk losing them again by feeding you money so you can get out of debt and spend as much as you want. Charles has had enough.' Nathan glanced back at Maisie and Noah. 'As for the assault and attempted kidnap on Maisie, your maid is going to be charged for that. If she ends up naming you as the person who set this up, I'm sure the police will want to talk to you.'

Aunt Lily shook her head. 'No! No, I have nothing to do with that!'

'Given what you've done to your family, we don't believe you.'

'It's a shame we can't charge you with the death of our mother,' Noah said. 'That is what you deserve.'

'But sadly, that was a long time ago, and there is no evidence to convict you,' Nathan continued as if Noah hadn't said anything. 'You'll walk out of court and likely point the finger at your brother. Which is what you will do.'

Maisie watched as Aunt Lily remained silent. She was clearly weighing up her options, trying to figure things out in her head. And she wasn't coming out with anything usable. Finally, she lifted her chin and straightened up. 'What do you want from me?' she asked. 'I'm not going to jail.'

This had been discussed in the carriage on the way over. Maisie stepped forward, surprised to find she was almost eye-to-eye with her aunt. She hadn't expected that at all. Aunt Lily was looking more and more frail now. That spurred her on.

'You can leave,' Maisie said firmly.

'What?'

'You can leave the area. Move anywhere in the country if you wish, but far away from temptation. You are to stay there and never come back to the area or contact your family again.'

Aunt Lily looked as if Maisie had slapped her. 'But...what about my husband? He's going to find out what's going on.'

'Tell him whatever you want, but you are leaving. And if anyone comes after me, Noah, or Father again, we'll go to the authorities and tell them exactly what you've done and how you used blackmail and attempted kidnapping to get what you wanted.'

'You wouldn't,' Aunt Lily whispered.

'Oh, we would.'

'But you're blackmailing me now!'

Maisie shook her head. 'We're keeping ourselves safe from your machinations. And given what you've done to us, this is justified.'

'Maisie.' Nathan took her arm and urged her backwards. He squeezed her shoulder before facing Aunt Lily again. 'We're not going to say anything to your hosts about this. That's up to you, if you keep it respectful. We'll happily tell Lord Kedleston the truth if you try to disparage us. Same thing happens with the police. All we want is for you to leave your family alone for good. Never contact them again. Do you think you can do that?'

There was a moment of silence as Aunt Lily spluttered, clutching onto her horse's reins to the point the horse wasn't happy about it and was snorting loudly. Finally, the older woman nodded, and she answered without looking at any of them. 'I'll do it. Whatever you want. Just don't tell anyone what I've been up to.'

'What are you going to tell your husband?' Nathan asked.

'I'll think of something. Just...don't tell him. He'll be furious, and I can't cope with that.'

'As long as you keep your end of the bargain, we won't have to.' Nathan took Maisie's hand. 'I think that's all we needed to do. Anything else from you two?'

'Not from me,' Noah said, moving towards the carriage. 'She's not worth any further words from me.'

'And you, Maisie?'

Maisie stared at the woman who had housed her for seven years, who had abused her and treated her like she was worthless, all so she could get her hands on money. She felt sick standing before her, remembering everything they had gone through in that time. If there was a way to go back in time to when things were good for her family before their mother died, she wanted that. Before Aunt Lily ruined it all.

'I hope you're feeling pleased with yourself,' she mumbled. 'You ruined a family with what you wanted and didn't care about the consequences. If you got the money. And what did you get as a result? Estranged from your brother and his children, and creditors after you. You're going to be looking over your shoulder for the rest of your life because of your actions.'

Aunt Lily sniffed. 'As if you're a paragon of virtue,' she sneered.

'No, I'm not. Nobody is, not even the most pious of people. But at least I know where the line is and stop before I get there. And you didn't even care about that. You just wanted for yourself, leaving the consequences for someone else. You're not going to get that anymore. All because you chose to kill someone who was in the way of what you wanted, and you used children to manipulate someone who loved you. If you can live with yourself after that, you're a pathetic excuse of a person.'

The older woman rolled her eyes, and Maisie realised that Aunt Lily was never going to learn her lesson. She was always going to think that money was the top of the pile for her.

Turning away, Maisie headed towards the carriage. There was nothing more she could say to her anymore, not when it was clear Aunt Lily didn't care.

For a woman of her age, she was certainly the most stubborn person Maisie had ever met.

CHAPTER 12

They were nearly back home when Nathan leaned out of the window and signalled to the driver. 'Can you stop a moment, Matthews?'

'Yes, sir.'

Noah frowned at him as the carriage slowed down. 'What are you doing, Nathan?'

'I thought Maisie and I should have a walk back to the house.' Nathan gave him a pointed look. 'You go on back to Bethany and explain what's going on. I've got a few things I need to discuss with Maisie.'

He hadn't spoken to Noah about his feelings for Maisie, but he suspected that his friend was more than aware of it. Especially from the way he saw Noah glancing between the two of them. The other man's expression cleared, and he nodded, shifting towards the door. 'All right. But don't be too long. Bethany is going to wonder where you are.'

'You don't have to worry about anything, Noah. I'll look after Maisie.'

Noah smiled, his eyes glinting. 'I don't doubt that part.' He opened the door and gestured at it. 'Out you go. Enjoy the sunshine.'

Maisie looked between the two of them, clearly confused. 'What's going on? I feel like you're talking in a different language, and I have no idea what's being said.'

'You'll understand shortly.' Nathan got out first and reached in to take her hand. 'Will you walk with me, Maisie?'

He thought she would turn him down, but then Maisie nodded and smiled at him. That smile made his chest warm with pride. He enjoyed having something like that aimed in his direction. Hopefully, that would happen more often.

Maisie climbed out, and Noah closed the door. He leaned out of the window and gave them a careless wave as the carriage set off.

Maisie turned to Nathan with a frown. 'Why did you want me to walk back with you? I'm going to be late getting back to work.'

'Bethany will understand. And I wanted to speak with you alone.' Nathan held out an arm. 'Will you walk with me?'

'It's not as if I've got any choice,' Maisie teased, slipping her arm through his. 'I suppose I can use the sunshine. It's nice enough weather.'

'Well, after what we've done, I think we need to clear our heads.' Nathan let them walk on in silence for a moment before speaking again. 'How are you feeling after that? Has it made things feel any better?'

'I don't know.' Maisie sighed as she leaned into him. 'I feel exhausted. It felt good to say all of that to her, to tell her she needs to get out of our lives, but I'm just so tired.'

'You did get a few knocks to the head yesterday, remember. I'm not surprised you're exhausted by it all. You're going to need plenty of rest when you get home.'

'I hope so. I'm going to struggle otherwise.'

'I'm sure Bethany will allow you to have some sleep when we get back to the house. You've been through a lot in the last few days.' Nathan looked at her, liking the feeling of her holding onto him. He could easily get used to it on a regular basis. 'Do you think you'll be able to get better with your father? Or is that something you're going to struggle with?'

'I haven't given it much thought just yet,' Maisie replied. 'After all, he only came back into our lives yesterday, and I'm scared he's going to disappear again. I haven't even comprehended that he's back yet. This is…it feels like everything's just been piled on top of me all at once.'

'I understand that.' Nathan kissed her head. 'You've been through a lot. It's only fair for things to just overwhelm you. Nobody is going to blame you if you want to distance yourself from it all.'

'I suppose. Although I doubt I would have any time to rest to get my head around everything.'

Nathan smiled. He made a mental note to say something to Bethany about it. 'I'm sure we can arrange that.'

'How so?'

'You let me deal with that.' It was now or never. Nathan didn't want to lose his nerve. He stopped and turned to Maisie, taking her hands in his. 'I've got something I want to talk to you about, Maisie. It's very important.'

'Is that why you wanted to have a private walk with me?' Maisie asked with a wry smile.

'Pretty much.'

'Why, though? Why couldn't this wait until we got home?'

'Because you would have gone about your business, or you would have gone back to sleep at Bethany's insistence, and I wanted to talk to you before I was unable to.' Nathan knew he was beating around, and he needed to be more precise. 'Sorry, I… I'm not very good at this at all. I've not done this before.'

'Done what before?' Maisie stared at him. 'You're beginning to get me concerned, Nathan. What are you saying?'

'I've not admitted that…'

The words were getting stuck in his throat. It was annoying that he was able to talk to the most awkward of clients, but when it came to Maisie, that was something else. And with Maisie staring at him like he had gone mad, it was even harder.

Groaning, he cupped her head in his hands and drew her close as he kissed her. Maisie made a sudden noise of surprise, but she sank into his embrace. Nathan was aware they were in public, kissing in the street, but he didn't care. He wanted this more, and it was worth the ridicule and the whispers.

They were both breathless when the kiss ended. Maisie stared at him, her cheeks flushed and her eyes bright. She had never looked more beautiful, and Nathan wanted to kiss her again.

'I…well…' She licked her lips, and Nathan had to stop himself from staring at her mouth. 'I don't know how to react to that.'

'Let's just say I've wanted to do that for some time now.'

'Really?' Maisie looked surprised. 'How long for?'

'Years. I don't even know how long, but years.' He stroked her cheek. 'I can't remember the moment I fell in love with you, Maisie, but I'm certain I've always been in love.'

Maisie's mouth opened and closed. Nathan laughed and tapped her nose with his finger.

'You look like a fish when you do that.'

'Oh, stop it!' She slapped his hand away. 'You can't say you love me and then call me a fish!'

'I thought it was sweet.'

'Well, don't call me a fish again.' But she was smiling as she said it. 'Otherwise, you're never going to get my response to what you've just said. Maybe I'll just walk away and leave you wondering if there is going to be anything between us.'

'What?'

With a wink at him, Maisie started walking away. Nathan groaned and hurried after her.

'Slow down, Maisie! That's not fair!' He grabbed her hand, Maisie laughing as he spun her around. 'I just laid my feelings out on the line, and you're walking away. Be kind to this man and put him out of his misery.'

Giggling, Maisie slapped his chest. Then she kissed him. Nathan didn't think he could smile any bigger.

'At least you're not bothered about being seen kissing in public,' he said.

'There's barely anyone around right now. And why waste an opportunity?' Maisie smiled back. 'It's certainly cheering me up after what happened the last couple of days.'

'I'm glad I can help you with that.' Nathan kissed her forehead. 'I love you. And I'm going to say that again and again, every day, to make you smile.'

'I'm sure you are.'

This was getting easier. Nathan had never admitted his feelings for anyone before, so doing it with Maisie had been even harder than his exams to become a solicitor. Now that he had gotten past that, it was one of the best things he had ever done.

'What are we going to do now?' Maisie asked. 'Isn't your sister going to be a little annoyed that you're in love with a servant?'

'If anything, she's going to be delighted. She was telling me to tell you how I felt only yesterday.'

'Really?'

'She loves you. She won't care if you and I get together. I think she'll be our biggest supporter.' Nathan kissed her. 'Besides, I think I've got a better position for you in that household. But you'll have to discuss the particulars.'

'Oh?' Maisie tilted her head to one side. 'What are you suggesting?'

'How does the role of wife sound compared to maid?'

It was not great as proposals went, but Nathan liked to bring something different to it. From the look on Maisie's face, she was thinking the same thing. Then she burst out laughing and flung her arms around his neck.

'I think that is something we need to discuss in greater detail,' she said as she kissed him. 'Once we get back to the house. Doing this in the street is probably not the best place for me to tell you that was probably the worst proposal I've ever heard.'

'That makes it sound like you've had plenty of proposals in the past.'

'No, but I know when it's a bad one.' Maisie grinned. 'I'll give you an hour, and then you can try again. How does that sound?'

Nathan groaned. Maisie was going to keep him on his toes, he was certain of it.

EPILOGUE

1896

Maisie smiled as she finished the letter. Nathan looked at her across the breakfast table.

'How's your father? Is he enjoying Hunstanton?'

'Very much so. I think he's found himself someone... interesting.'

'Oh?'

Maisie giggled. 'He's writing about a woman named Sarah, a widow who lives nearby. They've been spending a lot of time together, and he keeps mentioning her. It...it's clear that he's taken a fancy for her.'

'Ah, I see.' Nathan grinned, selecting a piece of toast from the rack. 'He's taken a fancy. And you don't mind?'

'Why should I? He's a grown man, and he's been a widower for fifteen years now. It's about time he had some happiness.'

It had been a surprise when Maisie started reading about another woman in the letters once Charles moved to Hunstanton, but then she had to remind herself that her father deserved some happiness in his life. He had been struggling for so long, thinking he had lost his entire family, so it was about time his luck changed.

Their relationship was going slowly. Maisie and Noah were still somewhat nervous about trusting someone who put his sister before them to the point their mother died, but they could see he had been manipulated by Lily. They agreed to take it slowly and see how things went. Plus, Charles had completely cut contact with his sister, so things were progressing well.

Maisie was glad of that. She wanted her father to be happy. They all needed it now.

'I wonder what Noah is thinking if he's aware of his father finding another woman attractive,' Nathan commented, buttering his toast before taking a bite. 'He's going to find it very odd for himself, I know that much.'

'Oh, don't be silly. Noah will be fine with it.'

'Really?'

'Father says Noah is the one encouraging it. I think being married to Beatrice has given him a softer and newer insight into things. It's quite sweet.'

Nathan laughed. 'I don't think I can describe Noah as sweet. But I'm not his relative.'

'You're his brother-in-law now.'

'Even then, sweet is not what I would call him.'

Maisie couldn't argue with that. But her brother had softened a lot since getting married. Beatrice had calmed him down and knowing that their aunt would never bother them again had been ideal in pushing that along. Maisie had certainly felt a lot of weight lift off her shoulders once she knew Lily would not bother them anymore.

Especially not after what they heard a few weeks before. Lily had moved to the Lake District and had almost immediately got involved with a gambling ring. She had been caught and arrested for helping to run it, so it looked like she was going to join her maid Charlotte in jail for a few years. Maisie had to shake her head when she heard about it. They had hoped being cut off from everyone would knock some sense into the woman and she would clean up herself, but things were not happening the way she expected. Lily was on a self-destructive path.

She doubted her aunt would clean herself up after the jail sentence was completed. It was a shame, but Lily wasn't someone who would admit she was in the wrong.

Maisie was content to leave her be. Things were brighter, knowing she wasn't around anymore.

'How are you feeling?' Nathan asked, sipping his tea before nodding at the food still on Maisie's plate. 'Are you able to get something in you? I know you said you've been feeling sick lately.'

'I think I can manage a little.'

'Did you see the doctor about it?'

Maisie smiled, putting the letter down. 'I did. He said it's fine, no problem at all. It's perfectly normal.'

'How is being sick perfectly normal? Are you sure that's what he said?'

She could tell her husband hadn't figured it out. She laid a hand on her still-flat stomach, waiting for him to notice. Nathan was an excellent solicitor and good at picking up subtle signs, but there were times when he needed it to be spelt out for him.

This time, he got the second hint. He looked up at her and then almost dropped his teacup. 'What? You're pregnant?'

'I am. The doctor says feeling ill is normal.'

'Normal?'

Maisie shrugged.

'The sickness didn't start for a while, so I was lucky. Just a few more months, and it should go away and be replaced with a baby.'

Nathan was beaming now. He got up and came around the table. Then he cupped her head in his hands and kissed her firmly. Both were smiling when he broke apart. Nathan's eyes sparkled as he then kissed her forehead.

'We're going to have a baby of our own.' He sounded like he was in a daze. 'We're married and having a baby, Bethany and Christian are in the next street with Noah and Beatrice working for them, and our parents are in good health…what more could we want in life?'

Maisie beamed back at him, linking their fingers on her stomach.

'I think we've got everything we need right here,' she replied. 'And it's just what I wanted.'

The End

If you enjoyed this story, could I please ask you to leave a review on Amazon?

Thank you so much.

Printed in Great Britain
by Amazon